The Bridge from Me to You

ALSO BY LISA SCHROEDER

I Heart You, You Haunt Me
Chasing Brooklyn
The Day Before
Far from You
Falling for You

FOR YOUNGER READERS

Charmed Life:
Caitlin's Lucky Charm
Mia's Golden Bird
Libby's Sweet Surprise
Hannah's Bright Star

It's Raining Cupcakes
Sprinkles and Secrets
Frosting and Friendship

The Bridge from Me to You

....

LISA SCHROEDER

....

Point

Library of Congress Cataloging-in-Publication Data

Schroeder, Lisa.

   The bridge from me to you / by Lisa Schroeder.

        pages cm

   Summary: "Lauren is the new girl in town with a dark secret. Colby is
the football hero with a dream of something more. In alternating chapters
they come together, fall apart, and build something stronger than either of
them thought possible — something to truly believe in" — Provided by
publisher.

   ISBN 978-0-545-64601-7

   [1. Love — Fiction. 2. Secrets — Fiction. 3. Football — Fiction.
4. Mothers and daughters — Fiction.] I. Title.

   PZ7.S3818Br 2014

   [Fic] — dc23

                                                    2013033112

Text copyright © 2014 by Lisa Schroeder

All rights reserved. Published by Point, an imprint of Scholastic Inc.,
Publishers since 1920. SCHOLASTIC, POINT, and associated logos are
trademarks and/or registered trademarks of Scholastic Inc.

10 9 8 7 6 5 4 3 2 1   14 15 16 17 18

Printed in the U.S.A.   23

First printing, August 2014

For Laura and Sarah,
my Texas forever friends

The Bridge from Me to You

Part 1

· · · · · · · · · · · · · · · · · · · ·

"If you were born without wings, do nothing
to prevent them from growing."
— COCO CHANEL

1 | Lauren

THE HOUSE smells like
apple pie thanks to the
burning candle on the mantel.

Uncle Josh and
my three cousins are outside
throwing the football around.

Apparently this small town
loves football
the way ducks love water.

Once in a while, laughter
drifts in through the open windows,
and I wish I could bottle it up
and carry it with me, letting out
just a little when I need a smile.

It's a strange, magical place, this house.

Aunt Erica is in the kitchen
making dinner, but every now
and then she pokes her head

into the family room,
where I'm watching a movie,
and says, "Oh, I love this part."

It's *Pretty Woman*, where the hooker
walks around the fancy hotel,
trying to fit in like
the only cat at a dog park.

Where I come from,
there were no scented candles,
no fun family games,
no savory Sunday dinner.

It was a strange, crazy place, my house.

How long 'til they notice
a cat like me doesn't belong
in a nice dog park like this?

2 : Colby

IT'S BENNY and me, tossing the football around in my front yard, like we've done at least a thousand times. But this is the first time we've done it before the first day of practice our senior year.

This is our last chance.

Our last chance to bring home a high school championship.

I look at my best friend standing across from me, sweat glistening on his muscular black arms, and I know for him, we have to win. Taking state may be the only chance he has at catching a scout's eye.

It's been a lot easier for me. How can he not hate me for that?

"You're so good, you don't even need to go to practice, do you?" Benny jokes as the football spins toward me. "I bet you just show up so Coach will make the rest of us work harder."

It's like he can read my mind. Maybe that's what happens when you've been best friends for what feels like forever.

"You know if there was any way I could skip out on two-a-days, I definitely would," I say as I take a couple of steps to make the catch.

"Drink lots of water tonight," he says. "Gotta stay hydrated, man."

I throw the ball back. "Aw, isn't that sweet. Big ol' Benny actually cares about me."

He walks toward me, half a grin on his face. "Just don't want you passing out. Remember that one time last year when about half the team went down? That was crazy."

"Yeah, I think it was about a hundred and ten degrees that day." I hold out my arms and look up at the clear summer sky. Weather-wise, this is about as perfect as it gets in Willow, Oregon. Not too hot, a light breeze now and then, and no rain for days. "It'll be all right tomorrow. I got a good feeling."

"Well, that makes one of us."

We walk up to the front steps of my house and take a seat. "What are you worried about?" I ask. "You got that guard spot cinched."

"I'll tell you what I'm worried about. Two words: Coach Sperry."

"I think his bark is worse than his bite. Especially right now. He's just trying to show us who's boss. You know, establish an order."

"What other order is there? He's the coach and we're the players. The end. We know where we stand. He's got an amazing team that almost made it to the championships last year. He doesn't need to do much except keep us on track. Let us do what we're good at."

"Colby," Gram calls. "Dinner's ready."

"You staying?" I ask Benny as we get to our feet.

He hands me the football. "Can't. Ma's expecting me home. Making my favorite tonight. Ribs and mashed potatoes."

"Jesus. You make it sound like it's your last meal or something."

"We got a new coach, man. Who knows what's gonna happen tomorrow."

"Well, aren't you Little Miss Sunshine." He shrugs, and I slap him on the back. "It's gonna be all right."

"Yeah. Ma always says when life hands you lemons, you gotta try your best to make lemonade. Nothing's ever perfect. There's always gonna be bad stuff to go with the good."

"Benny, Coach might be a great guy. I mean, maybe he'll lead us to the best year we've ever had. We don't know yet. We don't know anything. We just gotta wait and see, right?"

He waves as he walks toward his motorcycle. "Right. See you tomorrow. Bright and early!"

"Yep. You can count on that!"

3 : Lauren

WHEN THEY come in from outside,
smelling like sunshine,
Andrew, Henry, and Demi
pounce on me.

They are playful puppies
demanding my attention.

"Whatcha watching?"
"Can we watch too?"
"Who's that pretty lady?"
"What's she doing?"

I find the remote and change the
channel. SpongeBob is greeted
with more cheers than
a homecoming queen.

I go into the kitchen and ask
Aunt Erica if I can set the table.

"Thanks, sweetie.
I appreciate that."

She doesn't know I do it for myself
just as much as I do it for her.
I like setting six places
with her pretty dishes and silverware.
I've never been a part of making
something special like that.

Uncle Josh is sitting in his spot,
reading the Sunday paper.

"Two-a-days start tomorrow," he tells me
as he folds over the sports section.

"What's that?"

He explains how the football players
practice twice a day to get conditioned.

I remember Mom telling me a long time
ago that Uncle Josh, her brother, used to play.

"The new guy's supposed to be one hell of a coach,"
he says.

I don't know what to say,
so I just nod.

"You're gonna love your new school," he tells me.
"Just you wait. A great football team.
And a lot of school spirit."

I want to say school spirit
is the least of my worries.
Instead, I step back and admire
the beautiful table.

Erica calls out, "Lauren, would you mind helping me in
here, please?"

In a minute, we'll sit down in our spots,
pass around the serving dishes, and fill
our plates with food that's as new
to me as this small town of Willow.

"Coming," I say.

Josh looks up at me.
"You know, it's nice having you around."

I don't walk into the kitchen.
I float.

4 : Colby

"BENNY DIDN'T want to stay?" Gram asks. "He's more than welcome. We have plenty."

"No, his mom was expecting him home. Thanks, though. I know he appreciates the offer."

I take a seat as Dad comes in. "Smells delicious, Mom," he says.

"Spaghetti with meatballs. Have to make sure the athlete gets lot of protein and carbohydrates for tomorrow."

We start passing plates around, and I think about how Dad and I used to spend our Sundays. He'd go out and get a bunch of Chinese food. We never ate at the table. Instead, we'd kick back in the family room and eat in front of the television, watching ESPN.

Since Gram and Grandpa moved in a couple of months ago, things have been different. Gram loves to cook, or maybe she just loves seeing us eat, I'm not sure. I have to say, it's pretty nice having home-cooked meals all the time now.

After my mom died when I was two, Gram and Grandpa begged my dad to let them move across the country and help him. But he didn't want that. He said he could manage things on his own. I had a nanny until I was twelve, and after that I took care of myself. None of it ever bothered me, it's just how it was. It was my normal, I guess.

I look at Grandpa, who I haven't seen much today. "You feeling all right?"

He passes me the salad. "I'm feeling fine, Colby. Thanks for asking."

He's got MS, or multiple sclerosis, so some days are better than others. Dad finally invited them to come live with us when Grandpa's symptoms started getting worse. My gram was so relieved. They used to visit us a few times a year, and each time I could tell by the comments she made that she hated being so far away.

"Can hardly believe it's finally here," Dad says as he picks up his glass of wine. "The season we've all been waiting for. I can't wait to hear which college you choose, Colby. You know I'm rooting for Oregon, but of course, it's up to you. You've got three great schools interested, and really, you can't lose with a single one of them. You about ready to verbally commit?"

"Nope."

He smiles. "Gonna string 'em along for a while, huh? Make 'em sweat?"

"Nah, I want to get through this season, that's all. Then I'll decide. There's no hurry, right? I mean, signing day is still six months away."

Last year was pretty intense with college visits and meetings with recruiters. I'm glad the season's starting, so they'll be busy and might leave me alone for a while.

"Well, I'm telling you, a verbal commit would be a good thing."

I move my spaghetti around my plate. "But I'm really not sure yet. I just want to wait, you know?"

I look at him. His smile's gone. "Fine. Though I don't know what else you could possibly need to make a decision."

"More time, okay? I need more time."

"All right, then. Enjoy it. There's nothing more exciting than your senior year when you're a football player. I remember mine like it was yesterday."

I let out a big sigh. I'm tired of talking about this, and I don't want to pretend to be excited when I'm not. He's always just assumed I want to play college ball. He's never asked me, not once, about my feelings on the subject. Bugs the crap out of me.

"The spaghetti's really good," I tell Gram. "Did you do something different?"

"Why, yes, I did. I'm surprised you noticed."

Yeah, well, just because my dad is clueless a lot of the time, doesn't mean I am too.

5 | Lauren

AFTER DINNER, we head out back
for dessert.
Smoke wafts up from
the fire pit in the
middle of the patio,
and it smells really good.

The kids take turns
roasting marshmallows
on their sticks
and squishing them
between graham crackers
with squares of Hershey's chocolate.

"Do you want a s'more?" seven-year-old Henry asks.

I take the one in his hand,
smiling at the cobweb
of marshmallow covering
his little lips and cheek.

"Thanks," I say.
After I take a bite, I tell him,
"This is the best s'more I've ever had."

He bounces over
to the table of supplies
and starts the whole process
over again.

"Hey, kids," Uncle Josh says.
He puts his finger to his lips.
"Shhhh, listen."

We freeze in our spots.
The fire hisses and pops,
the only noise for a minute.

And then, we hear it.
A soft and eerie
whooo-hoooo
drifts down from the darkness.

"Is that an owl?" four-year-old Demi asks.

"What else would it be?" Andrew asks.
"An elephant?"

Andrew cracks me up.
How can you not love
a sarcastic nine-year-old?

Demi doesn't find it
quite as funny.
She reaches over and
slaps him on the arm.

Aunt Erica goes to work
making peace while I listen
for more soothing owl sounds.

When I was eight,
I visited my grandma down
in San Jose, California.
Her backyard was a bird
haven, with baths and feeders
in every corner.

She'd sit for hours on the deck
with her fancy camera,
zooming in on her little
feathered friends.

As I watched the birds
come and go, fluttering between
the big, open sky
and the welcoming yard
on sun-tipped wings,
I fell in love.

They were sweet.
They were beautiful.
And they could fly.

Oh, to be a bird, I thought.
To fly away and be free.

6 : Colby

IT'S MONDAY morning, a little before seven, and we're quietly padding up, getting ready to take the field.

"Gather round," Coach Sperry yells.

We hit the gym with the new coach in June and July, but this will be our first time on the field with him.

Half dressed, we do as he says. Coach walks around, handing each of us a small laminated card. I read the words. They're the same ones on the new sign hanging on the wall of the locker room.

> I believe.
> I believe in myself.
> I believe in the team.
> I believe it's our time.

A couple of guys chuckle. It does sound kind of corny.

"Come on, now," the coach says with his southern drawl. "This is serious stuff."

Benny leans in and whispers in my ear. "What is this shit? Do we look like a bunch of girls with confidence issues?"

Coach looks over at Benny and scowls. "Half the game is played up here," he says as he points to his head. "Now, you are an incredibly talented team. I know that and you know that. What we have with this team is a once-in-a-lifetime opportunity. It's not often when the planets align and the right talent shows up at the same time and forms a dynamic team. But that's what's happened with y'all. So we have to make the most of it, and not let your mental game be what defeats you.

"Each of you will stick this card in your wallet where you can see it. And you will read the words every day. I want you to come to practice ready. By that I mean ready to give me your best. But more importantly, ready to give your team your best. Are you ready?"

"Ready!"

"I believe," Coach yells.

"I believe," we reply, half-assed.

"What's that?" he says.

"I believe!" we yell.

"See you on the field in five," Coach says as he turns to leave.

Benny and I hustle back to our lockers. "You nervous?" he asks me.

"Do eagles fly?"

"You love answering a question with a question, don't you?" He slaps my back. "No, these Eagles do not fly, Pynes. These Eagles play football. And these Eagles are counting on you, bro."

Like I need to be reminded.

7 | Lauren

I WAKE up sweating.
The same dream I've had too many times.

A baby cries.
Cries for some food in his tiny, hungry belly.

I run through the house,
searching every room.

A baby cries.
Cries for someone to hold him.

When I come to the nursery,
I rip the crib apart, because he has to be there.

A baby cries.
Cries for me to find him.

I look and I look and I look until I realize the truth.
I won't find him. He's gone.

A sister cries.
Cries for the little brother she's lost.

8 | Colby

AFTER PRACTICE, I go home, where Gram has scrambled enough eggs to feed the entire team.

"Sorry, no toast this morning," she says. "We're out of bread."

"It's okay," I say before I drink the big glass of juice she's poured. When I'm finished I tell her, "I'll pick some up later for you. After practice?"

She shakes her head. "Why do they make you work so hard? I don't like it."

"It'll be all right, Judith," Grandpa says. "He's strong and healthy. The coach just wants the boys in great shape for the first preseason game."

Even though they've been here awhile now, it's still weird having them around. Before they moved in with us, I came and went and Dad barely paid any attention. He works so much, he's hardly ever here. I'm still trying to get used to curiosity and questions. And huge plates of scrambled eggs.

"You like the new coach?" Grandpa asks.

"He seems all right, I guess." I reach down to get my wallet and show Grandpa the card. "Every player got one of these this morning."

"Hm. I suppose he wants your head in the right place." He looks at me. "You think it is?"

I started as wide receiver last year. Our quarterback, Seth Temple, and I are a great team. I pretty much catch anything Temple sends my way. I'm not too worried.

"My head is exactly where it should be," I tell Grandpa before I shovel more eggs into my mouth. "Between my shoulders."

Gram chuckles as she puts her hand on my back. "Yes, it is. And you're going to do just fine."

When I've had enough to eat, I stand up. "I'm tired. Think I'll catch a nap before I head into work. Thanks for breakfast."

"You're welcome. We'll keep the television down so we don't wake you."

I smile. "Don't worry. After that practice, I think I can sleep through anything."

9 | Lauren

I THROW the covers off
and lie there, telling myself
it was just a dream.
    Just a dream.
        Just a dream.

He's fine.
Wherever he is,
    he's fine.

If I think too long
and too hard
about the other options,
I start sinking into a
pool of despair.
It's dark and cold there,
and I don't want to
d
r
o
w
n

I tell myself
what I need to hear.
     He's fine.
After all, it's up to me
whether I sink or swim.

I roll over and stare at the bookshelf
my aunt and uncle got me.
Enough books there for
a high school lit class
and I haven't managed to read
one.

I should.

Josh and Erica are the
proud owners of
Whispering Willow Bookshop.

Every night, they read
to their kids before bed.
Sometimes to all of them in a group,
sometimes one-on-one.
Every now and then,
I sit in and listen.

They are excellent
storytellers, using different
voices and lots of emotion.
But that's not the best part.

The best part is for a little while,
I forget who I am
and why I'm here
and everything that's happened
up 'til now.

It's like the story puts
my brain on pause.

I get up and grab a book.

Because I could use
a little   pause
about now.

10 | Colby

"HOW WAS practice this morning?" Mr. Weir asks me as we go in the back so he can show me the shipment of boxes that came in earlier. I work at AutoZone part-time, mostly stocking shelves.

"Fine," I say.

"Think it's gonna be a good year?" he asks.

"Yeah, I think so," I reply, mostly because that's what he wants to hear.

This is how it is for most people here. They ask about football before anything else. Every year, as the sun burns high in the sky, August brings a new batch of hope to our town. Hope for a championship title. It may not come packed in boxes, like auto parts, but it's there, and everyone feels it.

Especially the players.

For two and a half hours, I unpack parts and get them shelved. When I'm finished, Mr. Weir says that's all he has for me and I'm free to go.

I punch out, and since I have a little time to kill before practice, I head to Whispering Willow Bookshop down the street.

"Colby," Mr. McMann says from the counter when I walk in the front door. "Good to see you. How's it going? The team looking good so far?"

"You bet," I say, because there it is again. Hope. Can't escape it. "I think it's gonna be a great year."

"Awesome," he says. "You here for that book you ordered?"

"Yes, sir."

"What was the title again?"

"*Bridging the World.*"

He turns around to a shelf on the wall where orders are stored. He pulls out the book and sets it on the counter.

"This is gorgeous," he says, rubbing the cover. He gives me a curious look. "You interested in bridges, Colby?"

I feel my cheeks getting warm. "Nah. It's, um, a gift. For my grandfather."

Mr. McMann nods. "Ah. I see. That's nice of you. I'm sure he's going to love it."

I get out my wallet and give him some cash. While he rings me up, he says, "Did I tell you I have a niece who'll be at your school this year?"

"I don't think so."

He hands me my change. "Her name's Lauren. Came here from Seattle. Really nice girl. She's a little nervous about being the new kid. I keep telling her Willow High is a great school and she's going to get along just fine there."

I put my wallet away. "What year is she?"

"Senior. She's been living with us for a few weeks now."

I pick up the bag, wondering why she's living with them. I don't ask, though. None of my business. "Well, if I see her when school starts, I'll tell her hello."

He smiles. "Thanks. That's real nice of you." He nods at the book. "I hope your grandpa likes his gift."

"Thanks a lot."

There's a bakery in the far corner of the shop, so I walk over there. Quite a few people are sitting at tables, reading books or magazines. I get in line to order, hoping to avoid being recognized, because I don't want to talk about football practice or the new coach or how great this season is going to be.

In front of me, two women are talking. Not just any women, but women who walk around like they own the town. One is the wife of the best-known realtor in Willow, Mrs. Landry, and the other is a doctor's wife, Mrs. Poole. They both serve on the school board. My dad told me he's been to a couple of meetings, and apparently, they are not afraid of speaking their mind.

Even though they're trying to keep their voices down, I can't help but overhear their conversation.

"Well, I think it's strange," Mrs. Landry says. "You don't take a teen into your home when you have three small children of your own unless the circumstances are truly dire."

"What did he say again?" Mrs. Poole asks. "When you asked Josh why the girl is living with them? Word for word. What did he say?"

"He said his niece had a bad situation going on at home. So he and his wife offered to take her in for a time. That's how he put it. 'A bad situation.'"

"I bet she does drugs," Mrs. Poole says. "Or worse. Poor man. I bet he'll end up regretting that decision."

Mrs. Landry's about to say something else, but she suddenly gets the bright idea to take a look around to make sure no one's listening. I want to tell her it's a little late for that. I quickly turn my eyes toward the floor, but it's not enough to keep her from seeing me.

"Well, look who it is, Marianne," Mrs. Landry says. "Colby Pynes. Fancy running into you on the first day of football practice. Getting yourself a little snack, huh? I don't blame you. I hear they work you boys hard."

"Hello, Colby," Mrs. Poole says. "Why, my husband was just talking about the team this morning. Said he feels like this is going to be your year."

"I hope so," I tell them.

"Ladies, may I help you?" the clerk calls to them, and they walk up to the counter, saving me from having to say anything more. Thank God.

After they've ordered, they tell me it was nice running into me and take their coffees and pastries to a table, where they'll no doubt come up with a hundred and one more reasons why Mr. McMann's niece moved in with them. I'd bet money that not a single one of those reasons will be right.

I step up to the counter and order two scones and a bottle of water to go. Once I'm in my truck, I check the clock before I start flipping through my new book. It's three twenty, which means I have a little time to enjoy some peace and quiet before the second practice of the day starts at four.

The bridges transport me to a place where there is no small-town talk, and no football to worry about. For a few glorious minutes, anyway.

11 : Lauren

WHEN I got here a few weeks ago,
Josh and Erica gave me a shiny new
bicycle — sky blue with a fat seat
and wide handlebars.

They smiled at me
like they'd just given me
the keys to the sweetest ride
known to teens.

I wished I were six
with pigtails
and an endless imagination,
instead of seventeen
and filled with uncertainty
about this small town.

"It's called a Cruiser," Aunt Erica said.
"Isn't it fun? Now you can get yourself places.
Anywhere you want to go, really."

That first day,
I looked at my aunt and uncle

and my three cousins,
who live in the-middle-of-nowhere Oregon,
and thought the only place I might
want to go was to see the birds again
at Grandma's house in California.

That'd be one long-ass bike ride.
And besides, she didn't want me.
Said she wasn't prepared to take me
in for an "unknown length of time."

Like I was prepared to leave
for an unknown length of time?

Today's the first day I've ridden anywhere.
My maiden voyage is to Jiffy Mart,
to get myself some Bugles.

As I park my bike
and fiddle with the lock,
an old Chevy pickup,
black as night and covered in
at least three coats of wax,
pulls into the parking lot.

I watch as the guy gets out.
He glances at me, probably
thinking I'm twelve because
I've got a sky-blue bike
and one of my cousin's

baseball hats on to cover up
my unwashed hair.

God, he's cute.
Short brown hair that curls
at the edges, and eyes the
color of rich, dark coffee.

When I go inside, I see
him head down the aisle
at the far end of the store.
I find the chip aisle and grab
a bag of my beloved Bugles.

We meet up at the register.
He's carrying a loaf of bread
in the crook of his arm,
like a football, along with a
bottle of red Gatorade.

"Go ahead," he says.

"Thanks," I mutter.

I step ahead, but the woman
at the register doesn't even
acknowledge me.

"Hey, Colby," she says, smiling.
"How's it going?
Survived the first day, I see."

"Yep. Just finished the second practice."

I drop a dollar and a bunch
of coins onto the counter
and count out the exact amount.
The cashier can't stop looking at
bread boy, or Colby, or
whoever he is.

Guess I'm not the only one
who thinks he's cute.

With my Bugles in hand,
I scurry to my bike,
hoping to take off before
he comes back out.
But of course, that's not
how it goes for me.

No. I can't unlock the bike
because I can't find the key.
I'm swearing inside my head,
wondering why my life always
goes like this.

Nothing easy.
Nothing as it should be.
Nothing found, just lost all the time.

12 | Colby

"**IS THIS** yours?" the cashier asks me, holding out a small silver key.

"Mine?" I ask. "No. Must be that girl's. Want me to give it to her?"

She smiles. "Would you mind? Since you're going out there anyway?"

"No problem."

When I get outside, the girl is searching the pavement. "You looking for this?" I ask her, holding out the key.

She turns around and lets out a big sigh of relief. Though she has a Giants baseball cap on, I can see she's good-looking. Big green eyes, high cheekbones, and a real pretty smile. Her cheeks turn pink as she stands there, looking at me.

"Oh God," she says. "I dropped it in there?"

"Just left it on the counter." I walk closer and hand it to her.

"Thanks," she says. "Maybe that's why my aunt and uncle got me a bike, instead of a car. Losing car keys would be a lot worse."

When she says "aunt and uncle," I realize why I've never seen this girl before. "Wait a second. Are you Lauren?"

She looks at me funny. "Yeah. How'd you know that?"

"I was at Whispering Willow earlier today, and your uncle

was asking me to watch out for you when school started. You know, to say hi or whatever."

She groans. "He did? Well, that's kind of, um, embarrassing."

What would she think if she knew people were talking about her? Wondering what her story is and how she ended up here? Well, I'm not going to tell her. I'm guessing she'll find out on her own soon enough, anyway.

"Nah. Don't worry. He didn't mean anything by it. Just cares about you, that's all." I decide I should change the subject, so we don't end this chance encounter on a bad note. I point to her bag of Bugles. "Do you think it's weird I've never had those before?"

Her eyes get big. "You've never had a Bugle? You are missing out. Forget potato chips, these are the best snack food around."

"Yeah? So, are you waiting until you get home to tear that bag open?"

"I guess I could let you have one, but I'm not sure I should be handing out my Bugles to strange guys in parking lots."

"Oh man, I haven't introduced myself, have I? Sorry. I'm Colby. Senior, like you." I hold my hand out. She frees up her right hand by putting everything in the left and shakes mine.

"Good to meet you, Colby." She moves over to the curb near my truck and sits down. "Might as well open them now and show you what you've been missing. Nice truck, by the way."

"Thanks." I take a seat next to her. "Nice bike, by the way."

She looks at me like I've just insulted her. "Maybe if I was ten."

"No," I tell her, setting the bag of bread down next to me. "I'm serious. I like it. The thing is, when you ride a bike, it's like a two-for-one. You get some exercise *and* you get yourself somewhere."

She rips the bag open and starts putting the funnel-shaped munchies on her fingers. She turns and paws at the air. "Food and wicked claws. How's that for a two-for-one?"

"Okay, now I really want to try one of these."

She hands me the bag, and I take one and pop it in my mouth.

"Delicious, right?" she says before she sticks a claw in her mouth and eats it.

I look her in the eyes. "Thanks to you, I think my life is complete now."

"Yep. I know. Hey, you want to trade my bike for your truck? Two-for-one, just like you said."

I grimace as I get to my feet. My legs are killing me. "That's a really nice offer, but I think I get enough exercise."

"Well, if you change your mind, you know where to find me."

"At the convenience store, buying Bugles?"

"Yep. Pretty much. Stupid small town."

"Think of it this way," I say as I walk toward my truck. "If it weren't small, I probably wouldn't have met you today."

She laughs. "And your life would have continued to be incomplete?"

"Exactly."

13 : Lauren

THERE'S THAT moment
when you
get a gift
from a friend
with the cutest
wrapping paper
you've ever seen,
covered in
colorful cupcakes,
and you're wishing
that what's inside
makes you smile
as much as that
adorable paper with
the matching bow.

You open it
slowly,
savoring it,
your hopes
floating higher
and higher,

like a birthday
balloon.

And then
you see
it's
good.

Not just good,
but the best thing ever,
and it's exciting
and you're happy
and you're wondering
when you can sneak away
and spend some time with the
amazing gift.

Yeah.
Meeting him
and talking to him
was pretty much
like that.

14 | Colby

I DRIVE home thinking about Lauren.

The way her eyes sparkled when she smiled.

The sound of her laugh.

The easy way we talked, without one mention of football.

There's a creek party coming up this Saturday, and I realize I should have told Lauren about it. Invited her to come along. It'd be a chance for her to meet people, maybe make a friend or two before school starts. I almost turn around to see if I can find her and her blue bicycle, which probably wouldn't be too hard, but I want to get the bread home to Gram, like I promised.

When I pull up to our house, Benny's motorcycle is parked in the street, and he's sitting on my front porch. Waiting for me, apparently.

"Didn't I spend enough time with you today?" I ask him.

"I need your help."

Benny is a big guy, with muscles like boulders. Looking at him, you wouldn't think he'd need help with anything.

"What's going on?"

"It's my mom's birthday." He reaches behind him and grabs a grocery bag he was hiding. "Can you help me whip up a cake?"

It makes me laugh. "Whip up a cake? What, do I look like Rachael Ray? Also, why in the hell didn't you just buy one? Isn't it a little late to be doing this now?"

He stands up. "Nah. We got time. We aren't eating dinner until eight. And she doesn't like store-bought cakes. Hates 'em, as a matter of fact. It's the frosting, I think. So I thought I'd make her an angel food cake. I even bought some strawberries to go with it."

"All right. Come on. Let's see if Gram is willing to share her kitchen with two sorry-ass chefs like us."

Gram and Grandpa are sitting in the family room, working on a crossword puzzle they set up on a card table.

"Gram, I got your bread. And Benny's wondering if he can borrow our kitchen to make his mom an angel food cake."

"Fine with me," she says. "I've got a roast in the slow cooker, but the oven is free. Do you want me to help you?"

"Nah," Benny says. "I don't want to put you out. We'll be okay. I even bought the right kind of pan, since I wasn't sure if you had one or not."

"That's real sweet of you, Benny," Gram says. "I'm sure your mother is going to love it."

"If we don't burn the thing," I mumble.

"Knock it off, Pynes. We are going to make the best-looking cake you've ever seen."

"Judith, you should find these boys some aprons," Grandpa says. "Pretty ones with lots of ruffles. And be sure to get a picture — I bet the *Valley Times* would love to see what some of the Eagle football players do in their spare time."

"Don't tease them, Hank," Gram says. "It's not nice."

"Yeah, just tease Benny, Grandpa."

Benny drops the grocery bag and attempts to put me in a headlock, but I wriggle away before he gets the chance.

We're both laughing as I grab the bag and head for the kitchen. "Come on, big guy," I say. "Let's do this thing."

The kitchen smells amazing, with the roast cooking away, and my stomach rumbles. I set the bread I bought at Jiffy Mart along with Benny's grocery bag on the counter before I take out the cake mix and pan. I read the instructions and say, "Well, what do you know. It looks to me like you picked the easiest cake ever. We just have to add water to the mix and that's it." I look at him. "Why'd you come here? You could have done this by yourself."

He shrugs. "This way, if we somehow screw up the easiest cake ever, I can blame you."

I pull a bowl out of the cupboard. "You're such a good friend, Ben."

"I know it."

"You do realize I'm gonna have to follow you home when it's done, right? Unless you bought a special cake carrier for your motorcycle while you were at the store too."

He slaps himself upside the head. "Dang. I didn't think about that. You're right. But I'm guessing you don't have anything better to do tonight. Hey, you can even come in and have some cake with us. Ma would like that."

I have to say, I do love strawberry shortcake.

"Twist my arm."

15 Lauren

I TELL my uncle
I met Colby
at the store.

"Nice kid," he says.
"Great football player."

I'm glad about
the nice part,
but who cares
about football?

My cousins are playing
the most annoying
game in the history
of the world
with hippos and marbles,
so I take refuge
in the backyard.

As the sun begins
to set in the distance,
I listen for the

friendly owl,
but all is quiet.

Loneliness creeps in
and settles down
next to me.

I think of my friends,
Andi and Martina.
Do they miss me?
Do they wonder where I am?
Do they know I'm sick
about not saying good-bye?

I could call them,
but the thing is,
I know it'll make me
miss them even more.

It wouldn't do any good.
I'm here and they're not.

The ache in my chest
grows and grows
until I'm about ready
to go inside.

Right now,
annoying noise
might be better than
lonely silence.

But then, he's there.

whooo-hoooo

The haunting sound
of the owl's call
fills the empty space.

I close my eyes
and thank the owl
for talking to me
tonight.

My new friend learns
I'm a good listener.

16 : Colby

ON THE way to Benny's house, the warm wind blows through the open windows of my truck as the sun hangs low in the sky. Benny's in front of me, on his old Suzuki. He loves that bike almost as much as he loves football.

We drive through town, past the Hasty Freeze with a parking lot full of people. Past Purcell's New and Used Cars, where most kids get their first cars. And we drive past the Towne Pump, the gas station where we all meet up on Saturday nights, trying to figure out where we can find some fun.

As much as I think about leaving and moving on to bigger and better things, there are moments, like right now, when this small town makes me smile. It is home, after all.

When we reach his house, Benny pulls his bike into the driveway behind his mom's car. I park on the street, and then I grab the cake and strawberries.

I hand the cake off to him before we go inside. "Nice job, Rachael Ray," he says before he opens the door and yells, "Happy birthday to the best mother in the whole wide world!"

She peeks her head around the corner. When she sees him carrying a cake, she claps her hands over her mouth and comes all the way out from the kitchen.

"Benny. And Colby. What did you boys do?"

He walks over and hands it to her. "It's angel food. We made it ourselves. I got strawberries too."

"Oh my word, it looks wonderful." She looks at me. "You boys really made it?"

"Sure did," I say. "Happy birthday, Mrs. Lewis."

She sets the cake down on the coffee table, pulls Benny into a hug, and kisses him on the cheek. Then she does the same to me.

"Can you stay for dinner, Colby?" she asks. "The lasagna is just about ready. As soon as Ben's dad and brother get here, we'll eat."

"Ma, you shouldn't have cooked," Benny says. "We could have taken you out."

"I don't mind," she says. "As long as we're together, that's the important thing. So, Colby, you staying?"

"Yeah, my grandparents aren't expecting me home for a while. They know it's your birthday and that Benny and I wanted to help you celebrate."

"I just can't get over it," she says. "You boys doing this for me."

Just then, Mr. Lewis walks in the door. He's carrying a bunch of red roses wrapped in floral paper.

"Happy birthday, baby," he says as he hands her the flowers and gives her a kiss.

Benny motions to me to follow him into the kitchen, so I do.

"They like kissing each other," he tells me. "But that don't mean I have to watch."

It makes me laugh. "Well, it's good they love each other that much after all this time, right?"

"Right," he says as he flips through the pile of mail sitting on the counter. He flashes a couple of college brochures at me. "Since I took the SATs, they keep on coming."

"Hey, that's a good sign. Your scores must have been pretty decent."

"Yeah, I guess. Not sure it's gonna happen unless I get a scholarship, though. And I'm not talking one based on my academic achievements, if you know what I mean."

"Something will come through," I tell him. "Try not to stress about it."

I say it because this is what I want to happen for him. Maybe if we say it enough times, it really will.

"What about you?" he asks. "You made a decision?"

I sit at the kitchen table, and Benny joins me. I take a deep breath. "I know it's hard for people to understand, but I swear, I've thought about it a lot . . . and I'm pretty sure my mind's made up. I don't want to play college ball. I don't want the added pressure in college. The expectations. The baggage that comes with it, you know? I don't want professors to see me as the stupid jock. Or anyone, for that matter."

He squints his eyes like he's confused by my response. "But you're good, Pynes. I mean, do you know how good you are? It's like taking that beautiful and delicious cake we made, that we worked so hard on, and throwing it away. It's such a waste."

"As long as I go to college, isn't that the important thing? I mean, I played ball these past four years because it was fun, with you and the other guys. And around here, you know how it is."

"As my dad likes to say, it keeps us out of trouble," Benny says.

"Exactly. I'm glad I played. We all make a good team."

"Not just good, Pynes. A hell of a team."

"Yeah. But next year, it's a whole new ball game. The reasons I've loved it so much these past four years won't be there anymore."

"So how you gonna go without a football scholarship? Aren't you worried about that?"

I fiddle with a burgundy place mat in front of me. "I don't know. But I figure people do it all the time, right? I can get a job. Take out loans. My grades are really good; there might be other kinds of scholarships I can get." I look at him. He's trying to understand, but I also know he would give just about anything to trade places with me right now. And if I could, I would.

"And you know, it's important for you to remember that too," I tell him. "If you don't get a football scholarship, there are other ways. We can help each other figure it out, okay?"

"But I want to play," he says. "You probably don't even know how much I want to play."

He's right. I don't. Just like he doesn't know how much I'm ready to move on from living and breathing football.

His mom comes in. "Russ is pulling up. Can you boys get the table set, please? I just need to finish up the salad, then we'll be ready."

Both Benny and I stand up. I look at him. "For now, let's forget all that. Focus on the task at hand. To take state."

He reaches for a fist bump. "You can count on that." His eyes light up when he asks me, "Hey, after we eat dinner and have cake, wanna watch *The Avengers* again?"

I've lost track of how many times we've watched it.

"Is the Hulk green?" I ask.

"That would be a yes," he says.

And then Benny laughs. He laughs and laughs, like it's the funniest thing in the world. And then I'm laughing, and his mom is too. Happy birthday, for sure.

17 : Lauren

FOUR NIGHTS a week, Erica works
graveyard as a nurse at the hospital.

That way, the kids always have
a parent at home with them.

Sometimes Erica is asleep in the evening
when it's time for the bedtime routine.

But tonight both their mom and dad
are here for books and bedtime kisses.

"Want to join us?" Erica asks
as she gathers the kids to go upstairs.

I politely decline, because tonight
my heart is missing home pretty bad.

Maybe I didn't have a mom who
read books to me or tucked me in.

And maybe I wished for a mom who
liked to cook and gave long hugs.

But I never wanted this — to be
living somewhere else without her.

I miss our spa nights on Sundays,
with bottles of polish, a kaleidoscope of colors.

I miss the way she hummed, all the time,
but especially when she was nervous.

I miss passing the pint of ice cream
back and forth, like a special secret, between us.

I feel like I should try to let her go,
but if I do that, where does it leave me?

It's not like this nice happy
family is mine to keep forever.

"Good night, Lauren," Demi says as her
little arms, full of love, reach up for a hug.

Leave it to a four-year-old to show
me what I really want, most of all.

18 : Colby

TUESDAY AFTERNOON, I stop in at Whispering Willow Bookshop again, between work and the second practice.

"Hey, Colby," Mr. McMann says. "I heard you met Lauren. Kind of funny you ran into her after we talked yesterday."

"Actually, that's why I'm here. Some of us are getting together on Saturday. We're going up to the creek to swim, and I thought I'd see if she wants to come along. Does she have a cell phone?"

He shakes his head. "No, unfortunately she doesn't. She'll have to get a job if she wants one. We just can't afford one for her. You could call her at the house, though. Do you want the number?"

"Sure."

He grabs a pad of paper, and when he's finished writing, he tears off the piece of paper and hands it to me.

"Thanks," I say.

"You bet. Hey, did you give your grandpa the book yet?"

"Oh, yeah. Last night. He liked it a lot. Thanks again."

He smiles. "My pleasure."

"See ya later."

As I walk to my truck, I think about how I probably shouldn't have lied. Maybe Mr. McMann wouldn't have thought anything of my weird fascination with bridges. It's not like I had to tell him how far my fascination goes. Just because I bought a book doesn't mean he has to know about my list of the top twenty bridges I want to visit in my lifetime.

Last night, after looking at the book for a while in bed, I redid the list. I do that sometimes. Narrowing it down to twenty is about as hard as scoring a touchdown on a kickoff.

The top five stayed the same, though:

1. **Sydney Harbour Bridge**, Sydney, Australia — the world's largest steel arch bridge
2. **Brooklyn Bridge**, New York, NY — designated a National Historic Landmark in 1964.
3. **Tower Bridge**, London, England — it looks old and modern at the same time
4. **Chapel Bridge**, Lucerne, Switzerland — the oldest wooden covered bridge in Europe
5. **Millau Viaduct**, southern France — the tallest vehicular bridge in the world

A couple of weeks ago, Gram was asking Grandpa if he'd take her out for a picnic at a spot near an old bridge she'd heard about.

"I just love old covered bridges," she'd said. "There's something special about them, don't you think, Colby?"

It was kind of weird she'd asked me. I hadn't ever said anything to them about my strange fascination. But I agreed with her. And then she said something I'll never forget: "I've always thought a bridge is like a good friend, holding its hand out to help you along on the more difficult parts of your journey."

In one sentence, she described it so well.

I'm not sure where I'll be going when I leave here. But wherever I go, one thing's for sure: There'll be bridges along the way. Since I don't plan on playing football next year, they may be the only friends I have for a while.

19 Lauren

"Good to see you again," Dr. Springer says.

Maybe I'm supposed to say "you too," but I don't. What seventeen-year-old is happy to see her therapist?

"Have you been writing in your journal?" she asks.

"Yes."

"Tell me about that."

I shrug. "What do you want to know?"

"What kinds of things are you writing about?"

"Bugles. My blue bicycle. Owls. A cute boy. Dreams."

She tilts her head. "You're not writing about what happened?"

I shake my head and pick at a rough nail on my thumb. "No. I don't want to write about that."

"I think it will help," she says. "That's the whole point of the journal, right?"

"I'm not really sure."

"What kind of dreams?" she asks.

Of all the things I mentioned, of course she'd pick that one.

"Bad ones," I say. "More like nightmares, really."

"Tell me about them."

I don't say anything for a minute, debating about whether I should tell her the truth or make something up. I remember what she said the first time I came here. The only chance at this actually working is if I'm honest with her. I don't have to say a lot, if I don't want to, but what I do say should be the truth.

I take a deep breath. "I dream about my brother all the time. He's crying, and I can't find him. I look and I look and he's just . . . nowhere."

"Sounds like you miss him. Do you?"

I glare at her. "That's a stupid question."

20 : Colby

EVERYONE'S MOVING slower today. Of course we are. Everything hurts after yesterday. Coach is on our asses, yelling at us over and over, "Move, move, MOVE!"

I try to focus on the things I like about football practice.

Being on the field with all my friends.

Knowing I'm getting stronger.

The smell of grass and summertime and sweat.

It isn't much of a list, but it'll have to do.

It is a long two and a half hours. And then it gets even longer.

"Time for gassers," Coach yells.

I'm pretty sure we all want to moan, but we know better. Drills are always done at the end of practice. When we're all dog-tired and just want to take a cold shower and drink Gatorade, we have to push past the pain and fatigue and do the sprints. They suck, but they also work. They get us in shape like nothing else does.

We line up at the goal line, Coach blows his whistle, and in our pads, we sprint down to the other goal line and back, twice. When we finish, we get a minute to rest before we do it again. Coach tells us our time and that for the next set, we have to do it in ten seconds less, to make sure we aren't dogging it.

And so it goes. We do the drill over and over again, until guys are puking right and left. Not me, thankfully.

The torture finally over, Coach has us gather round and take a knee. I stare up at him, wondering if we're going to enjoy hearing what he has to say. He's a hard guy to read. The way he looks at us, it's like he loves us and hates us at the same time. And maybe he does. One thing's for sure, the khaki shorts and polo shirts he likes to wear remind us that Frank Sperry is really nothing more than a regular guy who loves football.

"Good work today," he says with a slight grin, telling us he really means it. "It'll get easier. You all know that. This is what it takes. I haven't done my job if you can walk off this field like you've played golf instead of football."

His eyes move from player to player. "It takes a lot to win football games, boys. You know what it takes, but it's my job to remind you every single minute we're out here. It takes hard work. It takes heart. It takes character. Every time you dig deep and pull something out when you don't think there's anything left, you've become a better football player.

"All right, see you back here this afternoon. I believe!"

"I believe!" we yell.

Benny helps me to my feet. When he lets go, my legs buckle and I start to fall. He grabs me and picks me up.

"I got you," he says. "Don't worry, man. I got you."

I add this to my list of things I like about football practice.

21 : Lauren

NO WAY.
Did that really just happen?
Colby called me.

Called
me!

When Aunt Erica
told me I had a phone call
and it was a guy,
I thought there was
a mistake.
Who would call me?
At this house?
And why?

After I said hello, he said,
"I went by the Jiffy Mart
earlier today, but you weren't there.
So I had to get your number
from your uncle Josh."

I was like, "You were looking for me?
How come?
Did I lose something else?"

Yeah.
I lost my freaking mind, that's what.
Could I have been any more ridiculous?

He laughed.
He said he thought I might want to go
to a party up at the creek this Saturday.

"Who all will be there?" I asked.

"A bunch of people," he said.
"And me. I mean, if you don't want to —"

"No, I do! How far is it?
Like, can I ride my bike?"

"Well, you could, but it's a long way out there.
I'm happy to give you a ride."

"Really?"

"Yeah, of course.
Pick you up at one?"

"Okay. Yeah. I'll be ready."

"Great. See you then."

This is the
best thing
that's happened
to me since
I left my key
on that
Jiffy Mart counter.

22 | Colby

IT SEEMS like Friday will never get here. But eventually it does, and everyone in the locker room is laughing and joking around because we have two days off from the annoying alarm clock, bossy coaches, and pain-in-the-ass drills.

I feel like I could go to bed and sleep all the way until Monday morning. But of course I won't. It's time to have some fun.

"You want to do something tonight?" I ask Benny.

"You bet. Let's meet up at Murphy's Hill. Maybe eight o'clock? I'll swing by Russ's first and see if I can get us some beer."

"Sounds good. See ya then."

I take my time walking to my truck. It feels like someone's chewed up my legs and spit them back out. A white Kia pulls into the lot and parks next to my truck.

When Meghan gets out, her long, beautiful legs are what I notice first. Damn. I try to remember how long it's been since I've even seen the girl. A month? Two?

"Hey there," she says when I approach her. "Dang, you don't look too good."

"Wish I could say the same about you," I reply.

She laughs as she flips her blond hair. "I've missed you too. Want to get a bite to eat or something? Catch up?"

I drop my bag of gear on the ground. "Thanks for the offer, but I just made plans with Benny. Sorry."

"Oh, come on. He'd understand."

"What are you doing, Meghan? It's Friday night. Is your boyfriend out of town or something?"

She walks closer to me. "There is no boyfriend, Colby. And like I said, I've missed you."

We went out for a few months last fall. Went to the Homecoming dance together and everything. But it wasn't long after football season was over that she told me she needed space. A few weeks later, I heard she was going out with some guy in Lansford. Star of the basketball team or something.

Funny thing, though, I wasn't too broken up about it at all. She's nice to look at and we had some fun times, but I didn't miss her that much. I think she liked being seen with me more than she actually liked me. Everyone said we made the perfect couple, but not in the important ways. Not in the ways that matter. I'm pretty sure I was just a jersey to her, a jock who made her feel good about herself as we walked down the halls of Willow High.

I don't want that again. I'm tired of doing things simply because other people think it makes sense. You know — because in Small Town, USA, that's what football players do; they go out with cheerleaders. Honestly, the last thing I want right now is someone worshipping me, up close and personal.

"Sorry," I tell her, "but if you need a shoulder to cry on because your heart is broken, mine is too damn sore right now."

"Well, here's a little secret. I'm your guardian angel this year."

I shake my head. "Wait. What? Meghan, you aren't supposed to tell me that. What are you doing?"

Every year, each football player is assigned a guardian angel from the cheerleading team. She bakes him goodies, gives him a gift bag with funny little gifts before every game, writes him encouraging notes after the game, that kind of thing. But it's all done anonymously, until the end of the season. The idea is that we each have someone "watching over us." It's supposed to bring the cheerleaders and the football players closer, and we have a lunch at the end for all of us. That's when we usually find out which cheerleader was assigned to each player.

But for some crazy reason, Meghan has decided she wants me to know now. Great.

She reaches up and touches my face for a second, before she says, "Look, let's not dance around, Colby. I basically came here to tell you, I'm here for you. If you need me, I'm here."

Dance around what?

And then I get it. Holy shit. I get what she's trying to say. And honestly, I'm speechless. Maybe some guys would be all over this. Maybe some guys would say, "Awesome, great, throw yourself at my feet because I'm one of the star players, and when I want a booty call, I damn well deserve a booty call."

But oh my God. What is she *doing*?

I pick up my bag and step away from her. "Meghan, thanks, um, for the offer, or whatever, but can we go back to the way it's supposed to be? You know, do the whole guardian angel thing anonymously? I bet you can switch with someone, right? Since school hasn't started yet?"

"Are you serious?" she asks.

"Yeah. I am."

"But I requested you specifically." She gives me a sad smile. "I know you aren't seeing anyone, and . . . you know. We were good together."

I can't even believe how messed up this whole thing is right now. Doesn't she know how pathetic this makes her look?

"Look, I'm sorry. Don't take it the wrong way, okay? You're a beautiful girl. But of all the things I need right now, this isn't one of them."

"Something's changed," she says. "You're different."

"Actually, Meghan," I say as I open the door to my truck, "I just don't think you, like most of the people in this freaking town, ever really knew me in the first place."

23 : Lauren

I WANT to go for a bike ride, maybe get some Bugles.
I'm about to yell to let Erica know, when I hear them
in the laundry room as I'm walking toward the garage.

"Erica, we haven't had a night out alone in over a month.
What's wrong with having a sitter?
She must have realized this would come up sometime."

"I don't want to make her feel bad.
I just don't think it's a good idea. Not yet.
Maybe after she's here awhile longer. We can wait. Please?"

I clear my throat and walk quickly, glancing as I go.
"Oh, there you are. I was looking for you.
"I'm gonna go for a bike ride, if that's all right?"

They nod and give their approval with their cheeks
flushed, like I caught them doing naughty things.
But really, I'm the naughty one in this scenario.

They don't trust me. They think I'm unbalanced,
and they can't imagine asking me to watch their precious
little children for a couple of hours because

what if something awful happened while they were gone?
I want to tell them I'd love to babysit and they would
not regret it, because I wouldn't let anything happen.

I adore those three kids, and I'd be a great babysitter.
But I don't say anything. I keep going. I get on my bike
and pedal fast and hard, one thought spinning like spokes.

They think they know me, but they don't.
They think they know me, but they don't.
They think they know me, but they really, really don't.

24 | Colby

AFTER I shower and eat dinner, I head up to Murphy's Hill to meet Benny. John Murphy was one of the greatest football players to come out of Willow. Rumor has it he wanted a place to party after games, so he went looking for a spot out in the country where he and his friends could have a good time without bothering anybody.

There's an old lumber road, nice and wide, off West Valley Road and it leads to a small hill with a clearing among all the trees. There's lots of space for cars to park along the road and there aren't any houses nearby. I didn't learn about the place until I got into high school, and that's the way it's always been, I think. It's become kind of this sacred place for students of Willow High.

When I pull onto the road, I make my way up toward the top. Since it's pretty early, there aren't any cars to greet me, though Benny's motorcycle is there. After I park, I grab the two lawn chairs from the bed of my truck. People either bring their own chairs or they stand, and I decided tonight was definitely a night we would want to sit and relax.

"Hey," I say as I approach Benny. "Your brother come through for us?"

"Nope. Wasn't home. And he didn't answer my texts. Sorry, man."

"That's all right. I'm so tired, probably would have just put me to sleep anyway."

We unfold the chairs and settle in. I take a deep breath, filing my lungs with the clean, fresh air that smells like earth and pine trees.

"Guess who I ran into in the parking lot after practice?" I say.

"Man, if you tell me the Hulk came by and I missed him, I'm gonna be really pissed."

I laugh, because neither one of us will ever get tired of bringing the Hulk into our conversations.

"Not the Hulk. Meghan Cooley. It was kind of ridiculous how she was throwing herself at me."

"Oh no. Hell no. You gotta stay focused on football."

"Wait a minute. At least half the players on our team have girlfriends right now. If they can do both, why can't I?"

"Because they're better football players than you, that's why."

I pick up a small stick and throw it at him. He catches it and throws it right back. "You're just jealous," I say.

"You know she's not my type. Look, I just think it's hard enough for you right now. Don't add one more thing to the mix. Get through the season, you know?"

"Yeah. Don't worry. I told her to get lost in the nicest way possible. It was not a pretty scene. I'll spare you the details."

"Well, good. No girls, Pynes. That's your motto. Got it?"

"So you probably don't want to hear I'm bringing a girl to the creek party tomorrow."

He shakes his head. "I'm telling you, a girl will just complicate your life, man. You don't need that."

"Maybe a girl would give me something else to think about besides football. I get sick of thinking about it all the time. Don't you?"

He leans back, puts his head in his hands. "Nah. Football is my escape. It's the rest of the shit I get tired of thinking about."

25 : Lauren

THE ONLY
bathing suit I have
is an ugly yellow
one-piece
that's two years old.
It hardly even fits.

Saturday morning
I'm trying to pretend
my aunt doesn't think
I'm a teenage delinquent
as I think about asking
if she has one
I can borrow.
She's tall and thin, like me.

I wish
    I hadn't heard them talking.
I wish
    I was a person they could be proud of.
I wish
    I had money so I could buy my own stupid suit.

Maybe I shouldn't go.
I could call Colby and tell him I'm sick.
Puking my guts out.
So sick I might be dying.

The truth is,
every day,
I feel like I'm dying inside
a little bit more.

I wish
      I hadn't messed up.
I wish
      it hadn't ever happened.
I wish
      we were all together again.

Henry and Demi barge
into my room
and beg me to play
blocks with them.

Today, I can play with
the little kids
or I can play
with the big kids.

I remember
      Colby's kind eyes and friendly smile.
I remember
      how he said he liked my bike.

I remember
    how he made me feel for five short minutes.

The big kids win.
I ask Aunt Erica for a suit.
She gives me a white bikini.

I put it on underneath
my shorts and T-shirt.

I've never been to a
creek party before.
Maybe people don't even swim.
Just in case, I want to be ready.

I remember
    swimming with my friends at the pool.
I remember
    flirting with boys and having fun.
I remember
    days when I felt alive and happy

and
I wish
    I could feel like that again.

26 : Colby

WHEN LAUREN greets me at the door, I almost fall over. I knew she was good-looking, but I didn't remember her being *this* good-looking.

I tell myself not to stare, but man, it is hard not to.

She's wearing a T-shirt and shorts, but a swimsuit strap tied around her neck tells me she has a suit on underneath. Her curly red hair falls around her shoulders, and her green eyes light up as she says, "Hi! Let me grab my bag and I'll be right out."

"Sounds good."

As I move toward my truck, Mr. McMann steps through the open garage door. "Hi, Colby," he says, extending his hand. "Good to see you. Thanks for inviting Lauren to go along with you today."

"No problem. Should be fun."

Lauren comes scurrying out with a beach bag over her shoulder. "I've got a towel, sunscreen, and sunglasses. Anything else I need?"

"Nope," I tell her. "I think you're good to go."

"Should we expect you for dinner?" Mr. McMann asks Lauren.

"I don't know." She looks at me. "What time do you think we'll be home?"

"I'll have her home by six," I tell him.

"Perfect. Have fun and drive safe!"

"Bye," she says as we hop into my truck. I wave and pull out of the driveway.

Once we're down the street, she leans her head back on the seat. "I can't tell you how good it feels to be getting out of there and going somewhere." She looks at me. "Other than the Jiffy Mart, I mean."

"Really? You're tired of the Jiffy Mart? But there's so much to see and do. It doesn't get much better than corn dogs, hot and ready to eat."

"What is it with boys and corn dogs?" she asks. "My convenience store meal of choice is nachos. You just can't go wrong with chips and processed cheese."

I point behind us, to the bed of my truck. "I brought along some sodas and snacks, but unfortunately, no nachos. I did get some Bugles for you, though."

"You did?" she says as she claps her hands together.

"I have never seen a girl get so happy about a snack food."

"Yeah, I admit, it's kind of insane how much I love those things."

"So, tell me something else you love. Because so far our conversations have been focused on food. Don't get me wrong, I definitely like to eat, but I'm thinking there's got to be more to you than Bugles."

She doesn't answer right away. Just stares out the window. "Let's see. I love sunshine." Pause. "Daisies." Pause. "Paint-by-number sets and blue nail polish." Long pause. "Bake sales, hot air balloons, and birds."

"Wow. That's quite the list. Bake sales?"

"A bunch of sweets, all for the taking, and the money is for a good cause. What's not to love?"

It makes me smile. "You are so right."

"And here we are, back to food."

I laugh, because it's true. "So, what kind of birds, exactly?"

She shrugs. "Any kind, I guess. I think I like them all. I want to go to college and become an ornithologist."

"A what?"

"Ornithologist."

"Is that anything like an orthodontist?" I tease.

She gives me a funny look, like she's not sure if I'm being serious or not. "Um, no. It's someone who studies birds. I'm thinking I could travel the world and research rare birds or something. Doesn't that sound like fun?"

"Yeah. Actually, it does. Anything involving travel sounds good to me. What colleges are you looking at?"

"Well, I haven't really started looking yet. I mean, with moving and everything, it's been . . . hard. There's still time, right?"

"Of course. Lots of time. Once school starts up again, you can use the College and Career Center for research. The two ladies who work there are really nice."

"Good to know. So, what about you? What makes you happy? Besides football and corn dogs."

"Actually, you can scratch football off my list." I'm kind of surprised by the words that come tumbling out before I stop them. But this girl isn't from around here. Her life doesn't revolve around football like most people I know.

"Wait. So you play, but you don't really like it?"

I take a turn onto Mill Creek Road. "Well, I love my team, of course. And it's had its fun moments, but after this year, I'm ready to be done with it. Time to think about other things."

"Like what?" she asks. "What do you want to think about?"

I can't believe someone is actually asking me this. As if there's something worth thinking about that isn't football.

I just might like this girl.

27 ⋮ Lauren

WHEN COLBY asked me
what I love, I almost said it.

I almost said his name. Matthew.
But I stopped myself.

Because then he would have asked me,
"Who's that?"

And I would have had
to say, "My brother."

More questions would have followed.
Questions I can't answer.

So I gave a list of things I love.
Even though I love Matthew most of all.

28 : Colby

"YOU'LL LAUGH," I tell her.

"No. I promise I won't laugh. It can't be any stranger than birds, can it? What kind of weirdo girl thinks about birds?"

"You're not weird."

"Neither are you. So tell me."

I take a deep breath. I've never told anyone what I'm about to tell this girl who I've known for a whopping five days. "Bridges."

"Bridges? Like in music or the kind you cross over because there's water?"

"Damn, I wish I was a musician, but no. The other kind."

"Huh. That's interesting. I don't think about bridges much. When you need one, it's just . . . there, you know?"

"Exactly. It's pretty incredible when you think about it. How could we get anywhere without them? But even more than that, there are some awesome bridges around the world. Like, there's this one in Switzerland that was built in 1333, and inside, it has paintings from the seventeenth century."

"Inside?"

"Yeah. It's the oldest wooden covered bridge in Europe."

"Wow. I've actually never seen a wooden covered bridge. Do they even exist here in the US anymore?"

I look at her. "Are you serious?"

"Yeah. Why?"

"If you want, we can go see one right now. Unless you're anxious to get to the party."

"I'm not anxious at all."

"Okay, then. I can't believe I get to show you your first covered bridge."

29 Lauren

Big blue sky.

Old country road.

Windows rolled down.

Insecurities left behind.
FlyingFlyingFlying   FlyingFlyingFlying
LovethisLovethis Warm breeze whispering. LovethisLovethis
FreeFreeFreeFree   FreeFreeFreeFree
Brown eyes sparkling.

Escaping the world.

Small lingering glances.

Nervous and excited.

Finally something good.

Sweet and sincere.

Hoping it's real.

Wishing it lasts.

30 : Colby

I TAKE the back roads until we come to it. I pull onto the shoulder, about thirty feet behind the old white bridge. She opens her door and hops out of my truck.

"God. It's so beautiful," she calls back. I watch her as she walks up the road until she's standing underneath the cover.

"I love how the sides are open so you can see out," she says when I join her.

"Yeah. It's called a Howe truss. William Howe came up with the design using diagonal beams in 1840. Because wood was less expensive, it could be used for the diagonal beams, while iron was only used for the vertical ones."

She takes a few steps and peers out between the diagonal beams. "What river is that?"

"It's Mill Creek, and up there a little ways" — I turn around and point — "is where Willow Springs River empties into the creek. It's not every day you see a river emptying into a creek. Pretty cool, right?"

She looks at me. "How do you know all of this?"

"Well, it's incredible, actually. There's this thing called the Internet. Maybe you've heard of it?"

She scrunches up her face and sticks her tongue out at me. It's kind of hilarious. "Ha ha," she says. "Okay, so maybe a better question would be, *why* do you know all of this?"

I shrug. "What can I say? I like bridges. And since this one is practically in my backyard, I wanted to know more about it."

"When was it built?"

"1939."

A breeze comes through, and it catches a wisp of her hair, blowing it across her face. She reaches up and tucks it behind her ear. I know I should turn away. Stop staring. But I can't. There is something so damn attractive about this girl and her curiosity.

"It's so quiet and peaceful, isn't it?" she says. "It's almost like we've stepped back in time."

"Come on. I'll show you something else."

We walk across the bridge, then down and around, through grass and past big trees, to a rickety waterwheel that sits on the edge of the creek.

"What is it?" she asks.

"A waterwheel power plant. It was used to power a saw-mill that used to be down here somewhere."

"It's not very big," she says. "I mean, shouldn't it be bigger?"

"I think this is just part of it. I'm not sure."

Just then, a robin lands on a branch not far from where we're standing. We don't move. The bird only sits there for a few seconds before it takes off, flying across the meadow behind us.

Lauren turns to watch it fly away.

I simply watch her. She is so mesmerized by that lonely robin; she looks like a little girl seeing a bird for the first time.

Guess I'm not the only one who thinks about flying away, to bigger and better things.

31 | Lauren

PARTY?
What party?
Let's stay here.
The two of us.
With birds and a bridge.

Imagine.
Two people.
Letting guards down.
Feeling happy and comfortable.
Never happened to me before.

Heart.
Beating fast.
Boy and girl.
Standing in the meadow.
It's like time has stopped.

Until.
Three words.
"Ready to go?"
Afraid to say no.

I'll never forget this day.

32 ┊ Colby

THE PARTY'S in full swing when we get there. People are spread out all over — some are in the creek; some are up by the rope, waiting for a turn to swing and jump; some are standing around, talking; and a few are sitting on the bank. We head toward the creek, since the bank seems like the logical starting point.

People say hi as we go along, and each time, I introduce Lauren.

We take a seat with our towels underneath us and the cooler beside us. Music's blasting from someone's car stereo. Lauren takes off her T-shirt, revealing a white bikini top underneath.

"I hate this," she says.

"You want to get in the water, then?"

"No, I mean, I hate being the new girl. It's so . . . awkward."

"Sorry," I tell her as I take off my shirt. I figure it's only fair. "Better here than in the cafeteria the first day, though, right?"

She gets her sunglasses out of her bag. "I guess. But still."

I turn and see Stasia a ways down. I know it's her because of her pink hair. When I see her sitting by herself, I remember that her best friend moved to Berkeley a couple of months ago.

"Stasia," I yell. "Come sit with us. There's someone I want you to meet."

I turn to Lauren. "She's kind of wild and crazy, but in the best possible way." She raises her eyebrows. I laugh. "Trust me, all right?"

Sure enough, Lauren and Stasia hit it off. When Stasia hears Lauren moved from Seattle, she asks if Lauren knows the band The Head and the Heart, who are also from there. Turns out it's one of her favorites. So they talk music for a while, until it gets hot and we're all ready to make our way into the creek and cool off.

As we're wading in, Stasia says, "This small town must seem so incredibly boring compared to Seattle. Why'd you move here anyway?"

Lauren looks down at the water, stepping carefully as she goes. "I needed a break from my mom. We were at each other's throats all the time, you know?"

"Believe me," Stasia says. "I know."

"So my uncle," Lauren continues, "who's my mom's brother, said I could live with them for a while."

"Her uncle is Josh McMann," I tell Stasia. "Owner of the bookstore?"

"Oh, right," she says, smiling at Lauren. "Super-nice guy."

Suddenly, Lauren reaches down and splashes icy cold creek water at us. Stasia screams. I react by seeking revenge.

"Oh no you don't," I say, grabbing Lauren's arm and pulling her down into the water.

Lauren wiggles out of my grip and pops up, laughing. She wraps her arms around herself. "You guys are crazy," she says, wading back toward the shore. "That water is freaking freezing."

"You started it," I remind her.

She doesn't deny it. Something tells me it was a strategic move on her part. After all, it's hard to ask personal questions when you're in the middle of a water fight.

33 : Lauren

IT'S BEEN my strategy
all along.

Anyone who asks, I simply
say I needed a break.

I twist things around
to make it about her, not me.

Sure, it's a bit extreme,
moving to a small town.

My only other option is
to say my mother died.

Nothing shuts people up
faster than death.

But the truth is,
I hope to go back soon.

I couldn't bring my mom
back from the dead.

But I could say I've decided
to give her another chance.

Of course, for me to say that,
she has to want to take me back.

She's not dead to me.
But what if I'm dead to her?

34 Colby

LAUREN'S SITTING back, eyeing the people doing the rope swing into the water.

"You want to try it?" I ask her.

"Only if you'll do it with me."

"Think that thing can hold both of us?" I ask.

"Are you trying to tell me something? Like, lay off the snack foods, maybe?"

I laugh. "No, no. I swear. That's not what I meant. All right, what the hell. Let's do it."

We make our way to the takeoff spot. I grab the rope with both hands as high as possible and tell her to grab below mine.

"What if I can't hang on?" she asks.

"You're wondering that now?" I tease.

"It's just, things look a lot different up here, you know?"

"You can do it," I assure her. "It's only a couple of seconds until we're over the water. Then you can let go."

"Okay."

"That doesn't sound very convincing. Say, 'I believe.'"

She gives me a funny look. "What?"

"It's something our team says. Come on. I believe."

"I believe?"

"One thing's for sure. You are not going to make it as a football player."

"You know, that's the best news I've heard all day."

How could I not like this girl? "Okay, smart-ass, do you want to do this or not?"

She takes a deep breath. "Yes. I want to. But, what if you land on me?"

"I won't land on you. You'll jump to the right side and I'll jump to the left, okay?"

"Okay. I'm ready. On the count of three."

We both count out loud. "One. Two. Three."

As soon as we say "three," we let the rope pull us out and over the water, our bodies hanging together, practically one. Lauren screams the entire way. Despite the possibility of damaging my eardrums, I love every second of being so close to her.

We let go at the exact same time, at the perfect moment. When we come up for air, I swim over to her.

"That was fun," she says, her face inches from mine, water streaming down as she wipes the hair out of her eyes. I have a tiny urge to kiss her right then, but I remain the perfect gentleman.

We swim a few feet to get to a spot where we can touch the bottom.

"I knew you could do it," I tell her.

"It was that pep talk you gave me."

"Yeah?"

"Yeah. It worked. You guys will be champions for sure."

"You gonna come to the games?" I ask as we walk ashore.

She shrugs. "I don't know. Football isn't really my thing."

Why is a girl who plays hard to get so damn attractive?

"Do you play offense or defense?" she asks.

"Sometimes both. But primarily offense, catching passes."

"Okay, how about this?" she says. "Promise to score a touchdown for me, and I'll come."

I turn to her and hold my hand out. "Deal."

She shakes it. "To one game. And to keep you guessing, you won't know which one I'm coming to. And I expect to see my touchdown in person. Because what fun is it otherwise?"

"Wait. So that means I have to score at every game?"

She smiles. "You said it, not me."

35 : Lauren

WHEN ONE of Colby's teammates
pulls him into the water,
leaving Stasia and me alone,
she says, "I think he likes you."

"I think he's just a nice guy."

"That too.
There should be more like him."

She then goes on
to tell me about
her last boyfriend,
who didn't know how
to keep his eyes
from wandering.

I tell her about
this guy I went out with
who didn't know how
to talk about anyone
but himself.

"You know it's bad,"
I tell her, "when he asks
where you want to eat
before the movie, and you
suggest TacoTime's drive-thru."

"To avoid face-to-face conversation?"

"Exactly."

We both laugh.

A friendship is born.

36 Colby

WE'RE ALMOST to her house.

I'm trying to figure out how I let her know I'd love to see her again. Like, go out for real or whatever. Because this was basically just a ride.

Wasn't it?

When I pull into the driveway, she turns to me and says, "Thanks. That was a lot of fun. Stasia said to give her a call and we'd get together, so I'm definitely going to do that. I'm so glad I got to meet some people before school starts."

I nod. "Good. I'm glad."

She waits, like she's expecting me to say something else. God, I hate this. My palms are sweaty. My legs are shaking. And my heart is beating like a freaking galloping horse. Asking a girl out for the first time is worse than being down six points with only fifteen seconds on the clock.

Because here's the thing every guy hates about this moment.

What if she says no?

37 Lauren

THE FEELING
in my stomach
as I jumped
from that rope
is nothing
like the feeling
in my stomach
as I sit in his truck
and wait to see
if he's going to
ask me out.

After a few
awkward seconds,
I can't stand it anymore
and say,
"Guess I'll see you around,"
as I open my door.

"You bet.
Maybe I'll see you at the Jiffy Mart."

As I walk toward
the front door, it feels
like someone has tied
a rock to my heart
and dropped it into
that creek.

Disappointment
bubbles up
to the surface
and I realize I
should have asked
him to call me.

I turn around,
hoping to correct my mistake.

But he's already gone.

38 : Colby

DID I really just say that? "Maybe I'll see you at the Jiffy Mart"?

What the hell, Pynes? She was right there. Right there, waiting for you to say something, *anything*, about the fun afternoon or how you loved hanging out with her or maybe you could get together again sometime. And you failed. Miserably.

Third down with two yards to go, and you blew it. Couldn't get it over the line and had to punt it away.

I'm a disgrace. A disgrace to senior guys all across the country.

I think it was Benny's fault. All of his talk about how I have to forget about girls and stay focused on football right now messed with me. I bet I internalized that, and even though I wanted to ask her out, I couldn't because deep down somewhere, I feared he was right.

As I think about Benny, I realize I never saw him at the creek party. He said he'd be there. I went home last night after a couple of hours at Murphy's Hill, as lots of people were arriving. I was dead tired and just wanted to go home to sleep, but Benny didn't want to leave yet. He was wide-awake and having fun.

I pull out my phone as I walk in the front door.

"Hi, Colby," Gram calls out. "Dinner will be ready in about fifteen minutes."

"Okay. I'm gonna take a quick shower." Maybe I can wash the embarrassment away.

First I dial Benny's number. But it goes straight to voice mail.

If he's out with some cute girl, I will be so pissed.

39 Lauren

I HAVE three choices:

1. Wait to see if he calls me.
2. Call him.
3. Move into the Jiffy Mart.

40 : Colby

GRAM KNOCKS on the bathroom door just as I'm getting out of the shower. "Colby? You need to come out here. Hurry."

My first thought is Grandpa. Something's happened to Grandpa. I don't even dry off; I just grab a towel, wrap it around my waist, and pull the door open.

"What is it? What's wrong?"

She motions me to the family room, where Grandpa is sitting, watching the news. I rush over to him. "Are you all right?"

He points to the television, and I turn to see a picture of Benny on the screen. His football picture from last year. My heart stops.

". . . in critical condition at Willow General Hospital."

The camera switches to the reporter, standing in front of the hospital. "The accident happened at around one thirty a.m. Saturday morning on West Valley Road. Police say Lewis was on a motorcycle, and failed to negotiate a curve. The motorcycle crossed the center lane and slid over fifty feet, causing Lewis to lose control. Investigators say Lewis was wearing a helmet, though it may not have been fastened securely as it was found nearby at the scene. Doctors say Lewis has suffered severe head trauma, and his injuries are life threatening."

She keeps talking, but I don't hear what she says. Because I can't believe it. I can't believe this is happening.

"I have to try calling him again," I say. "Someone's made a mistake. Someone needs to tell him what's going on so he can clear this mess up."

"Oh, Colby," Gram says, tears in her eyes. "I'm so sorry. It wouldn't be on the news if they weren't a hundred percent sure it's him."

Grandpa stands up. "Go get dressed. I'll drive you to the hospital."

"But, Grandpa —"

"I know. Damn it, I know. Just go get dressed."

I can't move.

I can't breathe.

Finally, Gram comes over, puts her arm around me, and leads me to my room.

"I'm going to call the church," she tells me. "They'll start a prayer chain for him."

She closes the door.

I grab my phone and dial his number.

"You have reached the Life-Model Decoy of Tony Stark. Please leave a message."

"Benny. Call me. Please? Please. You need to call me."

Part 2

· · · · · · · · · · · · · · · · · · · ·

"He will cover you with his feathers,
and under his wings you will find refuge;
his faithfulness will be your shield and rampart."

— PSALM 91:4

41 : Lauren

TUESDAY

"Lauren, what's new?" Dr. Springer asks. "How's school going?"

"I don't know. I guess it's all right."

"What's the latest on the boy in the hospital?"

"I heard some kids talking today, and they said Benny came out of his coma. I hope it's true."

"Last time, you spoke of a boy you met. What was his name?"

"Colby. Turns out he's Benny's best friend."

"Any luck talking to him? How's he doing?"

I look out the window. It's a pretty September day. Nice and warm. I wish I were outside, sitting in the sun, instead of in here. "I don't know. I haven't talked to him."

"Well, you may want to reach out to him. People hurting need to know they have friends who care about them."

Surprisingly, I think she's right about that.

"Have you been writing in your journal?"

I sink down into my chair, as deep as I can go. "Not lately."

"Do you still have the nightmare?"

"Yes."

"Are you ready to talk about what happened?"

I don't know why, but this question pisses me off. I scowl

at her. "I don't get why I have to talk about it. I just want to try and forget about it."

She leans in, her voice soft but firm. "Lauren, traumatic events aren't just forgotten. It doesn't work that way. That's why you're here, so I can help you. I want you to be able to live a full and happy life, but before that can happen, we have to work through your feelings about what happened. You need to find some closure."

I reach up and rub my temples. "I hate this." I feel tears welling up. "You know, it's all her fault."

"Whose fault?"

I glare at her. "You know who. My mother."

"Okay. Let's start there. Tell me about her."

I sigh and tick things off on my fingers. "She has really thin hair, nothing like mine. She loves pizza. But no olives. She can't stand olives. Oh, and she loves watching that hoarding show." I shudder. "I have no idea why."

Dr. Springer smiles. "Do you think she's a good mother?"

I smirk. "There's definitely room for improvement."

"Even so, she's your mother, right? And I'm guessing there are some things you like about her?"

She won't make me cry.

She won't make me cry.

She won't make me cry.

"Yes. And sometimes I miss her so much I can hardly stand it. Then other times I find myself hoping that I never have to see her again. I just don't understand . . ."

I look out the window, willing the tears back.

"What, Lauren? You don't understand what?"

I say it so softly, I'm not sure she can even hear me. "How she could have done that to me."

42 | Colby

AFTER OUR second grueling practice of the week, Coach gathers us around before releasing us for the day. He's got his clipboard in one hand; his other hand sits in the pocket of his khaki shorts. It's like he's trying to look relaxed, but I can tell he's really not. It's been a difficult few weeks. For all of us.

"Last Friday night, we got lucky," he says. "We should not have won that game. You know it and I know it. That's why I'm working you so hard this week. Look, I know it's difficult, not having Lewis here, playing with y'all. But if anything, that's more of a reason to want to win. Don't let yourself down. And for God's sake, don't let him down. Get mad! And then go out on the field and put that anger to good use. You know Lewis wouldn't want it any other way.

"Before the game on Friday, we'll have stickers for your helmets with Lewis's number, sixty-two, on them. I'm sorry it's taken so long for them to get here. I know he's on your minds, but the game must go on. And this time, it won't be enough to simply show up. You've gotta want it, and play like you want it." He looks at me. "You can do this. I believe!"

"I believe!" we reply with as much enthusiasm as we can find, which isn't much.

"Nice work today. See y'all tomorrow."

The other guys scramble to their feet and hustle off to the locker room, anxious to get home. Eat. Do homework. See their girlfriends.

They are so different from me. All I want to do is find a hole, crawl into it, and sleep for a hundred years. God, I'm tired.

Since the accident, when I'm not at work or on the football field, I'm at the hospital. Of course, now school has started, so I have that to deal with too. I haven't been allowed to see Benny, since I'm not family, but I wanted to be there, anyway, as much as possible.

Other friends came by to show their support for Benny. Coach came by a few times too. We'd talk a little, and when we ran out of things to say, we watched cartoons in the waiting room, or we'd go and get some bad food in the cafeteria. A lot of times, though, it was just me, sitting there, wishing things were different.

I can't stop feeling like it's partly my fault. Why didn't I pick him up and take him up to the Hill? I should have known that the old country road with its twists and turns is not something he should have been navigating on a bike at night. Usually when we go up there, we ride together, in my truck. Why did we do things differently? Why wasn't he with me, like he should have been?

There's been all kinds of speculation about what happened. Everyone I know says they'd left Murphy's Hill already. I don't understand why he was there so late, and maybe even the last one to have left. As for the accident, a lot of people wonder if he swerved to avoid hitting something coming at him, like a deer. Or maybe even another car, although no one has come forward with any information. The thing is, Benny loved that bike, and he was never careless. Ever. That's why it's hard to understand. It's as if trying to figure out why it happened will help them deal with it better. I get it.

When my mind won't let me sleep, thinking about Benny, I search for similar stories on the Internet. I want to know that he can recover from this. That he'll be okay. Sometimes, I find the kind of stories I'm looking for, where people come back after a traumatic brain injury. And sometimes, I find the kind of stories that remind me how fragile life is. How lucky Benny is to even be alive. It's shocking how many people die from motorcycle accidents. I had no idea.

I wonder if Benny knew. If he cared.

It's a vicious cycle of madness. We should have, he shouldn't have, why didn't he, why didn't I . . .

The fact is, it happened. And there's no going back.

Now, I get to my feet and drag myself to the locker room. I think about last night, when Benny finally came out of the coma. The doctor talked to his immediate family, and then Mrs. Lewis came to talk to me. I was so relieved that he'd finally woken up. When days turned into weeks, it was hard not to imagine the worst, though I tried not to let my mind go there very often.

The two times he had surgery to relieve the pressure in his brain, I sat in the chapel and prayed. What else could I do?

"Is he going to be all right?" I asked Mrs. Lewis when she sat down next to me and told me the news. That he'd finally woken up.

"There's still a lot we don't know," she said. "We have to wait and see. It could be a long, hard recovery." She tilted her head. Looked at me with nothing but love in her eyes. "Colby, I know this whole thing is eating you up. I can see it all over your face. But you listen to me. You have been a fine and faithful friend. You have nothing to feel guilty about. Nothing to feel bad about. Whatever happens now is out of our hands. He's a strong kid. A fighter. Hold on to that, have faith, and then, let the worry go."

I got that funny feeling in my throat, and I choked the tears back. I didn't want to cry. Not when I needed to be strong. Strong for her.

"I don't know how to do that," I whispered.

She pulled me into her arms. "Oh, honey. You have a life you need to live. It's time to learn."

43 | Lauren

COLBY NEVER called me,
like I hoped he would.

Once I learned it was his
best friend who was
the one in the coma,
it made sense.

I ran into Colby in the hallway
on the first day of school.
I stopped. Smiled.
Said, "Hey, good to see you."

"You too," he replied,
hardly looking at me
as he kept on walking.

Stasia said it's just how
guys are. They get stressed
out easier than girls.
They do what they have to do
to keep it together.

I keep trying to think of
something I can do to
cheer him up.

My mom used to call me
Sunny Bunny,
because I was always trying
to cheer her up.

I can't help it.
I hate seeing people
I care about sad.

And every time
I see Colby, it looks like
someone's told him
all the bridges
in the world have burned
to the ground.

44 | Colby

I HEAD home after practice because I have homework I've been neglecting. I tell myself that if there was news, good or bad, Benny's mom would have gotten in touch with me. It's probably still too soon to know what lies ahead.

Gram and Grandpa are surprised to see me for dinner. Lately, I've been coming home after they're in bed and I just heat up a plate of leftovers. But not tonight.

"You've lost weight, Colby," Gram says. "You're not taking care of yourself."

I sit down, and my stomach growls because I'm starving and everything smells delicious.

"I'm okay, Gram," I tell her as she passes me the bowl of mashed potatoes.

I'm about to say something else when Dad walks in.

"Oh, how nice," Gram says, getting up to set another place. "We're all here together for a change."

"Good to see you, Paul," Grandpa says.

"How are you feeling, Dad?" my dad asks Grandpa as he takes a seat.

"I'm doing just fine."

Dad turns to me. "Colby, how was your day? Hopefully life's a little easier now that we know Benny's out of the woods."

Easier? Give me a break. "It was fine, I guess."

"With the good news, maybe you guys can play a better game come Friday, huh?"

I stuff a big bite of mashed potatoes into my mouth so I don't tell him how little I care about football right now.

He dishes up his steak, salad, and potatoes and then looks at me. "Son, I know this has been rough on you, but you have got to try and put it behind you. You have to stay focused when you're on that field. Benny's a strong kid. He's gonna get through this. And you worrying about him doesn't do him or you a bit of good."

"Yeah. But it's hard, you know?"

His eyes are kind when he says, "I know. But right now, there's no room for error on that field. Until you sign a contract in February, anything could happen."

I don't say anything.

"I'm just looking out for you, Colby."

This is where I should call bullshit.

This is where I should tell him I'm tired of him reliving his glory years through me.

And this is where I should tell him that I don't want to play college ball. I want to go to college to study civil engineering, and that's my number one priority.

Instead, I say, "Yeah. Okay." And then I shovel more food in my mouth.

45 Lauren

I'VE APPLIED for a job at eight places,
and only one has called me for an interview.

On Thursday, I put on some nice clothes.
"Remember," Josh says, "smile a lot."

I tuck his piece of advice into my pocket
and ride my bike to King's Doughnuts.

As I pedal, I go over the list of things
I know about doughnuts.

They smell good, and they taste delicious.
And that is the extent of my knowledge.

I decide maybe it isn't so much what I know
about doughnuts but more about

customer service and how effective
I could be at selling baked goods.

*"Would you like to try our fall favorites,
apple cider or pumpkin spice?"*

*"If you buy a dozen doughnuts,
we'll give you one for free."*

*"Two doughnuts? You can't buy just two.
As soon as they're gone, you'll wish you had more."*

In the end, I'm not asked what I know
about doughnuts or how I'd sell them.

I'm asked about my strengths and weaknesses,
my grades, my schedule, my goals.

I discover interviewing for a job is like
taking a test you haven't studied for.

When it's over, I have no idea if I passed or failed,
but I say thank you and buy a dozen doughnuts.

46 Colby

WHEN MRS. Lewis calls me Thursday night, I'm thinking about all the normal things people are doing while Benny's lying in a hospital bed, his future uncertain.

They're eating pizza. Watching lame reality shows on television. Griping about too much homework. While they go on with their lives like nothing in the world is wrong, some people's lives will never be the same.

I want to punch something because of the unfairness of it all.

"We had a little bit of good news today," she tells me. "Benny touched his head. The doctors called it a purposeful movement, and they said it's a very good sign."

I lean back on my bed and breathe a sigh of relief. "Has he said anything?" I ask her.

"No. Not yet." She pauses. Takes a deep breath. "Colby, the fact of the matter is Benny has massive traumatic brain injuries. His prognosis at this time is unknown. We need to be patient and see what happens in the coming days and weeks. The doctors have told us to be prepared for a long road of recovery."

"Like, how long?"

She doesn't say anything for a few seconds. I know she's trying to keep it together, for my sake. "Honey, we're talking months. Maybe even . . . years. We just don't know."

I swallow hard. "Thanks for calling me. I really appreciate it."

"There's one more thing I want to tell you," she says.

"What's that?"

"You play hard tomorrow night," she says. "You think of Benny, and you win that game, just like he'd want you to."

"You know there's nothing I wouldn't do for him," I tell her, tears in my eyes.

"I know."

"And we're gonna win that game."

"I know."

47 Lauren

THE KIDS have matching
blue-and-gold knit hats
they wear to the football games.

Doesn't matter if it's not
very cold out. Blue and gold
are Eagle colors.

"You like wearing those itchy hats?"
I asked the kids last Friday
as they got ready to leave.

"They're not itchy," Demi said.
"They're soft."

"Do you like watching football?" I asked.

"Yes," they said in unison,
their heads bobbing up and down,
like three little parrots in a row.

"You want to go?" Erica asked me.

"No, thanks," I said.
"I've got homework."

Tonight they're getting ready again.
They've got their seat cushions,
their animal crackers,
and their itchy hats.

Demi comes over to the couch,
where I'm sitting.

"Come with us," she tells me.

"Well, you know, I would,
but I don't have a hat to keep
my head warm."

Demi pulls hers off. "You can wear mine."

"Actually," Erica says, "Lauren has her own."

She tosses a plastic bag in
my lap. I reach in and pull out
a hat just like the ones
Andrew, Henry, and Demi wear.

Demi jumps up and down.
"You've got a hat, you've got a hat,
now you can go, now you can GO!"

I tear the tag off and stick
the hat on my head.
It fits perfectly.
And Demi's right.
It's not itchy at all.

In fact, I'm pretty sure it's
the most awesome hat
I've ever owned.

48 : Colby

IT'S AN away game in Lansford, about a twenty-minute drive, which means most of our fans will make the trip to watch. As annoying as it gets to have everyone talk football with me everywhere I go, the support we get on game nights is incredible. Once in a while, I wonder if I'll miss that — knowing you have a whole town on your side.

In the locker room, Coach passes out the round stickers with Benny's number and tells us to hold the helmet with the face guard against our chest and place the sticker on the right side.

I know it's all about showing that we love and support him, but the thing is, I don't want to play with a sticker of Benny's number. I want to play with *Benny*. And the stickers remind me that I will probably never play with him again. And that right there is enough to make me want to run away and never come back.

But of course, I don't. I told Mrs. Lewis we'd win, and I have to somehow put all my feelings aside and go out there and play.

"I want you to remember something," Coach says. "Football is about defending what's ours. Let's go out there and defend our territory, like we do every game. But tonight, and every night for the rest of this season, let's defend our friend and teammate Mr. Benjamin Lewis. We will not let our guards down, for him. We will play with confidence, for him. We will play our best, for him. I believe!"

"I believe!" we yell.

"Now go out there and make him proud."

49 Lauren

THE GAME of football,
according to Uncle Josh:

Four downs
to move the
ball at least ten yards.

If you make it,
you get another ten,
and so on until you score.

If you don't,
you punt it away
and the other team
gets the ball.

The game of football
according to me:

Boys in weird-
looking pants
running around,
throwing a football,

and jumping on
each other.

Colby is number twenty
and he's who I watch
the most.

He misses pass after pass,
and in the third quarter,
there's an interception
that makes the crowd groan.

On the bench,
Colby puts his head in
his hands.

Never in a million years
did I think I'd feel like crying
at a football game.

50 | Colby

IT'S NOT that I don't want this win. I do.

I always want the win. There is pure magic in that moment when you look back and see what you did, sometimes against all odds, to come out ahead. Day in and day out, we struggle: with homework, with test scores, with parents, with teachers, with girls, with friends — some days, it seems, with *everything*. And we are usually alone in those daily struggles.

But on the field, when we struggle, we do it together. There is no greater feeling than knowing you have a team that is behind you one hundred percent. All working toward the same thing. All playing with heart and grit and passion, to make it through the crap and to come out the other side successful.

I love this team. I love what it feels like to be *part of* this team. When I'm on the field playing, most of the time, whatever's going on in my brain takes a backseat and the desire to win for my team takes over.

Tonight, I'm trying so hard, and yet, Benny's absence is there, following me like a shadow. It's worse than any defense coming my way. Nothing's going right. I'm a step ahead or a step behind, and once, I even let the ball slip through my fingers.

"Shake it off," Temple says to me when we huddle up in the third quarter. He slaps my helmet. "You can do this. We can do this. All we need is a first down. Focus on that right now." He calls the play; we clap and break.

As the football spins toward me, I see an image of Benny that day in my yard, tossing the ball around. It was a time when possibilities seemed endless and things were just as they should be.

The defender comes out of nowhere. My sixth sense must not be working, and when he intercepts the ball, it's another missed opportunity.

Another moment I can't get back.

Another thing taken from me.

I leave the field, disappointment swallowing me whole. Right now, troubles seem endless and things are not as they should be.

The question, of course, is what am I going to do about it. I know I've got to find something to hold on to. When I look up into the stands, I take a deep breath.

Because maybe, just maybe, I've found it.

51 Lauren

FOURTH QUARTER,
We're down by six.

Number twenty goes
back in to play.

Everyone stands
and cheers.

"Eagle" *clap, clap*
"Power" *clap, clap*

Colby sprints
down the field

with two defenders
on his tail.

"Eagle" *clap, clap*
"Power" *clap, clap*

He makes a turn
as the ball spins his way.

He jumps,
leans, s t r e t c h e s,

giving everything
he has to catch that ball.

"Eagle" *clap, clap*
"Power" *clap, clap*

The other two players try
to get in on the action too.

When the Eagle lands,
he's just inside the end zone,

and he's clutching the ball
like it'll break if he drops it.

Teammates give him pats
of adoration and appreciation.

When the kick is good,
the scoreboard shows

the Eagles in the lead. Joyous
screams erupt from the stands.

The game ends a
few seconds later and

in that moment I feel like
I'm a part of something magical.

I search the night sky for enchanted
stardust, swirling and whirling,

but all I see are tiny dots,
dim and dull compared to the

bright and shining stars
on the field this happy night.

52 | Colby

I SAW her in the stands. Lauren. The girl I wanted to get to know better until my world shattered into a million pieces.

After the interception, as I headed to the sidelines, I glanced up, and there she was. She and her cousins were hard to miss in their matching blue-and-gold hats near the front of the crowd.

Maybe I should have talked to her when she stopped me in the hall that first day, but when your heart is so full of pain and sadness, it's hard to make room for anything else. So I told myself to let her go. Besides, she didn't need me bringing her down.

But as I sat there on the bench, cooling off, I thought about our day together. About our walk back in time at the covered bridge. About our swing from the rope. About what she'd said.

Maybe if you score a touchdown for me, I'll come.

I told myself if I got another chance, if I got back in the game, I'd do things right. I'd think about her, believing in me enough to dare me to score a touchdown not just once, but once every *game*.

And then I realized she wasn't the only one who believed in me that way. Benny did too. I had to stop feeling sorry for myself and start being the kind of person he'd want me to be.

Seeing her there . . . it helped. It helped me a lot. It gave me the push I needed, and thankfully, I caught the pass when it really counted.

After the game, as I'm walking toward the team bus, Coach pulls me aside.

"I'm sorry," I say before he has a chance to get a word out. "About how I played most of the game."

"Son, I don't want your apology. What I want is the dedication and commitment you showed on that winning catch every minute you're on the field."

"Yes, sir."

"Your heart is heavy. I understand that. But when it's game time, you've got to find a way to leave it all behind and make the game the priority. There will be times in your life when things happen and you wish you could stay in bed for days, but you can't because people count on you. This is one of those times. Your team is counting on you now. As hard as it is, you've got to trust me that making you get out there and play is the best thing I can do for you right now."

"I know."

He slaps me on the back. "Enjoy your weekend. And son, if you need anything, you be sure and let me know, all right?"

"Thanks, Coach. That means a lot."

"Well, you mean a lot to this team. Remember that."

Once I'm on the bus, I put on my headphones, sink back into my seat, and close my eyes. Game over. Week over. My feelings for Lauren? Obviously, not over.

53 Lauren

FEAR IS like a mountain,
looming large
in the background,
taunting you with its
magnificence.

It seems so much
bigger than you,
and the thought of
climbing it,
of overcoming it,
seems impossible.

But it is not you
against the mountain.

The mountain does
not exist simply
to make you
feel small.

It exists for purposes
beyond your
understanding.

To climb it is simply
to take one step
and then another
step and then
another step;
a walk uphill.

It is all in how
you look at it.

And when you reach
the top, there is no more
mountain.
Only a view that
takes your breath
away.

I am afraid
to reach out
to this boy
I really like.

But I tell myself
it is not me
against the mountain.

I will not let it
make me feel small.

I can do this.
I can take one step
and then another
step and then
another step;
a walk uphill.

I tell myself
the view
will be worth it.

Completely
and totally
worth it.

54 : Colby

WHEN THE bus pulls into the school's parking lot, I think how this is where Benny would lean into me and say, "Whatcha up for now, Pynes?"

Sometimes it was Murphy's Hill.

Sometimes it was Angie's Restaurant and the all-you-can-eat pancake special with scrambled eggs and bacon.

Sometimes it was simply two words: "I'm beat." Benny had different ways of responding to that, and almost all of them made me laugh.

We trudge off the bus, and Derek Nelson asks me if I want to join him and a few other guys who are going to check out a party they heard about.

"Thanks, man, but I'm heading home. I gotta work tomorrow."

Derek looks over my shoulder and smiles. "Sure you do, Pynes. Sure you do."

I have no idea what he's talking about. I turn around and see Meghan leaning up against my truck.

"Damn," I say.

He slaps me on the shoulder. "Have fun."

I think about changing my mind and asking him for a ride to the party, if he'll bring me back here later. That's how much I don't want to talk to Meghan right now. But they're hooting and hollering and happy, walking across the parking lot, and I'm just not up to it.

"Good game," she says when I approach. "That catch at the end was brilliant."

"Thanks. I came through when it mattered, I guess." I move past her, and throw my bag in the bed of my truck.

She pulls on my arm, and when I turn around, she's right there. "I know you need someone right now." Her eyes are so sad. And for a second, I wonder why. What does she have to be sad about? "This thing with Benny is killing you, I can tell. Let me help you."

I sigh. "Meghan, I thought we already went over this."

"I'm not your guardian angel anymore, but that doesn't mean we can't . . . you know."

"Don't do this."

She looks surprised. "Do what?"

"This. Throw yourself at me because I'm the hero of the game tonight or whatever. Did you see the way I played the rest of the game? I'm not a hero. I'm so far from a hero, it's not even funny."

She looks heartbroken. "Colby, I like you. That's all."

I shake my head. "No. Like I told you before, I don't think you even really know me. What you like is being a part of the winning team. It makes you feel good. Because you obviously don't have much else in your life that makes you feel good about yourself, or you wouldn't be showing up here, acting like this."

Her eyes narrow. "You know what? You're wrong. I do know you. I know that you're an asshole." She stomps over to her car. "Jesus, I just felt bad for you and everything you've been going through. I wanted to *help* you!"

She gets in her car and speeds off before I can respond. Not that I have anything else to say.

Sometimes things in this small town are so backward, I can hardly see straight. I stand there, trying to think of one thing I actually like about this town right now.

And that's when I think of the girl who is so different from everyone else. The girl who'd never seen a covered bridge. The girl who doesn't really like football.

It's so cliché, but right now I feel like this small town might smother me, and Lauren is a breath of fresh air.

I want to see her. I want to remember what it's like to feel normal again.

So I get in my truck, and I head toward the Jiffy Mart.

55 : Lauren

JOSH AND Erica
let me go with
Stasia after the game.

She has a white
Ford Focus instead of
a blue bicycle.
We ride back
to Willow, singing
along to the radio.

A Katy Perry song
comes on, and I think
that they seem like
kindred spirits,
with Stasia's pink hair
and crazy clothes
and how she loves lollipops
(grape is her favorite).

There is something
about singing with
a girlfriend in the car,

happy and carefree,
that makes you
feel like you can
do

ANYTHING.

I tell myself I can
do what I want to do.

What I'm afraid to do.

What I need to do.

I can talk to Colby
when he gets off
the bus and tell him
I had so much fun
that day we spent
together and I've
missed him.

Maybe he feels
the same, maybe not,
but I want to know.

I need to know.

Stasia parks in a
dark corner, and

we wait for the bus
to arrive.

"He's really cute," she says.

"I know."

"I hope it works out."

"Me too."

She reaches into
the glove box to get
a lollipop. She offers
me one, but I decline.

The butterflies are
circling, and I tell myself
it's because I'm
excited, not nervous.

We watch as
a beautiful girl
walks up to
Colby's truck
and looks inside
before she turns
around and leans
up against it,
her arms crossed

like she's ready to
wait all night.

"Who is that?" I whisper.

"Meghan Cooley," Stasia says.
"His ex."

Suddenly, I'm wishing
I would feel afraid again.
Or nervous.
Or excited.
Anything besides the
sadness that fills me.

I can't believe
it's going to end
like this.

"Do you want to stay?" she asks.

"No.
I can't watch."

"I'm sorry," she says.

The story
of my whole
miserable life.

56 ⋮ Colby

I LOOK for her bike when I pull in, but of course, it's not there. Like I really expected her to be riding around this late on a Friday night?

Crazy, wishful thinking. There's no way I could be so lucky as to catch two breaks tonight.

I go inside to get a slushie, and as I turn the corner, there she is, Bugles and a soda in hand, waiting in line to pay at the register.

I freeze.

What do I do?

What do I say?

Lauren raises the bag, as if to say, no surprise, right?

Stasia comes up behind her, holding a tray of nachos. This is so awkward. I'm about to turn toward the slushie machine, where I can hide for a second and collect my thoughts, when I see Lauren hand Stasia her stuff and whisper something to her.

Then Lauren walks toward me.

"I can't believe I actually found you here," I say.

She looks surprised. "You were looking for me?"

I swallow hard. "Yeah. I was. I, uh, I saw you at the game. When Coach pulled me out."

She nods. "You made a touchdown. After that, I mean."

"I did." I motion toward the door. "Could we talk outside for a minute?"

"Sure."

I go to the door and hold it open while she steps out. I follow her down to the far corner of the store, where it's kind of private. And dark.

She has her arms crossed over her chest. "Are you cold?" I ask. "We can sit in my truck, if you want."

She smiles. "No. I'm okay."

I stick my hands in my pockets, in case they start shaking. "Look, I owe you an apology. I've had a lot going on, and, uh, I think I probably gave you the wrong impression."

"Oh," she says, her smile gone. "Well, you don't have to apologize. I mean, it was just one day and it was probably wrong to think —"

"Wait," I say. "No, that's not it. I meant, I think I've given you the wrong impression *recently*. Like, made you think I don't want anything to do with you, but it's not that at all. It's just, this whole thing with Benny . . ."

I think I see relief on her face. I hope I see relief on her face. "Oh, right. No, I get it. I mean, it's gotta be hard."

"Yeah. It is. I wish you could have met him. He's a great guy."

"Well, hopefully, someday I can. He can recover from this, can't he?"

"Absolutely. It could take a while, but yeah."

"That's good."

"Anyway, I'm sorry. If it seemed like I was ignoring you or whatever."

Before she can respond, the door opens, and we both

turn. Stasia looks around, and when she spots us, she calls out, "I'll be in the car."

Oh God. I can't make the same mistake twice. It's now or never. "Before you go," I say, the words tumbling out like a ball off a bad kick, "would you want to go out with me? Maybe tomorrow night? Or, you know, whenever you're free, I guess."

Lauren shakes her head, like she doesn't understand. "Wait. So what about that cheerleader?"

"What about her?"

"I saw her, waiting for you at school. You're not . . . together?"

"Oh, no. No way."

She gives me a little grin. "Well, that's a relief."

I nudge her with my elbow. "You weren't jealous, were you?"

I think she's trying to play it cool. "What? No. I just didn't know what was going on, that's all."

"Okay, good. Because I promise, there's nothing to worry about. So, are you free tomorrow night?"

"Yeah. I work tomorrow afternoon, until six. Can you pick me up at seven?"

"Where are you working?"

"King's Doughnuts."

"Oh, man, I love their doughnuts. That is a sweet job, Lauren."

She chuckles at my bad pun. "Real funny." She points toward Stasia's car. "I should probably get going. I'll see you tomorrow night."

"Yeah. Seven o'clock. Don't eat dinner, okay? I want to take you to my favorite restaurant."

She points at the store. "If you bring me here for corn dogs, I'm going to be totally insulted."

I laugh and raise my right hand. "No corn dogs. I swear."

"Okay, then. See ya later."

I watch as she hurries off to Stasia's car. Then I lean against the building and exhale. I'm finally on a winning streak.

57 Lauren

HIGH FIVES,
giggles,
and Bugles
thrown around
the car
like confetti.

"What are the chances?" Stasia asks
as we drive around the corner
to a little park, where we get out
to eat our snacks.

I'm the one
who asked her
to stop at Jiffy Mart.

Maybe he was
going to make out
with that hot girl,
but if not, maybe
he was going to stop
and get something to eat

because football players
are always hungry.

I figured I had a
fifty-fifty chance.

But I don't tell
Stasia that.

We sit on the swings,
side by side,
like little kids.
"I guess it was meant to be," I say.

She sighs.
"That is so romantic."

"Right," I say,
"because a convenience store
just screams we belong together."

"A match made in snack-food heaven," she says,
laughing.

"And guess what?
He told me he *loves* doughnuts!"

"Oh my God.
He is the perfect guy for you."

I think so too,
and I'm so excited
I get a chance to see
if we're right.

58 | Colby

DAD'S STILL up when I get home, watching TV and drinking a beer.

"Hey, Dad," I say. "Everything all right?"

He narrows his eyes as he looks up at me. "If you think playing a pathetic, sloppy football game is acceptable, sure. Everything's fine."

I set my bag down and take a seat in the recliner, where Grandpa usually sits.

"Yeah, I had a rough start. Just couldn't stop thinking about —"

"Colby, three quarters is not a *start*. There are no excuses for how you played. None."

I look down at my lap. There's nothing to do now but sit here and take it.

"I think if I were your coach, I'd ask you to hang up your jersey and let some other kid take your spot. Hell, a sixth grader could've played better than you did tonight."

Shame fills me. "I told Coach I was sorry."

"And what did he say?"

"He said he didn't want my apology. That what he wants is my dedication and commitment."

"Of course he does. The question is whether you want to give that to him."

I rub my face in my hands. "At least I made the play that mattered the most. Doesn't that count for something?"

"Yes. But come on, *every* play matters when you're out there this year. Every. Single. Play. What if scouts were watching tonight? Do you think any of them are going to want to have anything to do with you now?"

I look at him. "I can't think about that, Dad. I got enough going on without thinking about that too."

"Well, you need to find that commitment your coach wants to see somehow. Do you want to let him down?"

"No."

"What about your team? Do you want to let them down?"

I sigh. "No."

He stands up. "What time do you work tomorrow?"

"Uh, noon to five. Why?"

"You take your gear, and you meet me at the field after work."

I stand up. "I can't. I have a date."

He picks up the remote and turns off the television. "That's right, you do. With me. On that football field. No girls right now, Colby. Do you hear me? You said it yourself. You've got enough going on."

"But, Dad —"

"No. I'm not gonna back down from this. This is for your own good. You have to trust me on this. We need to get your head in the right place, and right now, that means more time on the field and less time thinking about other things. Like the opposite sex."

I can't believe this is happening.

He slaps my shoulder. "After we run some plays, you and I will go out for dinner. How's that? I know, we'll go to Fresh

Grill. Haven't been there in ages. Get one of their big, juicy burgers, huh? I'll tell Gram and Grandpa not to expect us tomorrow night. We'll have a fun night out, just you and me. Like the old days."

He pulls me into a hug. Squeezes me hard. I stand there, like a board. "I love you," he says. "Don't forget that. I know you're not happy with me right now, but this is the way it has to be." He pulls away and holds both of my shoulders with his hands. "Just for a few months. That's all. Okay? If this girl has any decency about her, she'll understand. And she'll wait."

I swallow hard.

"Good night," he says as he turns to leave. "I'll see you tomorrow. Five fifteen. Ready to play."

59 Lauren

MOONLIGHT SPILLS
into the front window.

Demi sleeps in her
mother's arms

as they rock to a
silent lullaby.

"She had a bad dream,"
Erica whispers to me.

I wonder what
that's like, to be

comforted by a loving
mother when you

are awakened by
frightening dreams.

I walk over and stroke
Demi's soft blond hair.

"Can I take her
to her room?" I ask.

I long to hold her,
to cuddle her,

to feel loved and needed
if only for a moment.

Without hesitation,
Erica stands and passes me

the sleeping angel.
Demi nestles in my arms,

as if she belongs there,
but of course, she doesn't.

She is a temporary solution
to a constant longing.

I go to bed knowing
I'll dream of him again,

and will wake up with
no one to comfort me.

60 | Colby

BENNY'D PROBABLY say I need to grow a pair and tell my dad where to go when he gets like that. But I can't. Because the thing is, I know my dad thinks what he's doing is for the best. Yeah, it's kind of tough love, but it's love all the same.

When you get down to it, he's right. I did play a pathetic, sloppy game. I had one good play, where I got lucky, and that's it. I love my team and I'd do anything for them. Like, I would never screw up on purpose, but I wonder if deep down, there's a part of me that realizes if I play poorly, my problem about whether I play football or not next year is easily solved.

I don't know. But I'm gonna do what my dad tells me to do because that's what I've always done. It's been him and me for so long, I don't know any other way.

On my way to work Saturday, I stop off at King's Doughnuts, hoping she's already started her shift. When I walk in, she's busy helping someone, so she doesn't see me. When I finally catch her eye, I smile and she smiles back.

All I can think is, *Please don't let her hate me for this.*

When the customer is done, I step up to the counter.

"Hi," I say.

"Hi. Can I get you something? A maple bar maybe? Or are you an apple fritter kind of guy?"

"I'll take two of those pumpkin spice," I tell her.

She raises her eyebrows. "Really? Well, what do you know, a guy after my own heart. Those are my favorite."

As she bags up my doughnuts, all the nervous feelings I felt last night come rushing back. It's crazy how much nerve it took to ask her out and now I have to find even more, except this time, there's nothing good waiting at the end of it all.

She hands me the bag, and I give her a five-dollar bill. "Lauren, I have some bad news."

As she gives me my change, her smile disappears. "Oh no. Is it Benny?"

"No, nothing like that. It's just, I have to cancel. I can't make it tonight. Something's come up. I'm really sorry."

"Oh. Right." She crosses her arms. "I'm sorry too." She pinches her lips together like she's deciding if she should say more. I wait, because I don't know what else to say. "Can we reschedule?" she asks.

God, I want to say yes. I almost say yes. But what am I gonna do, lie and sneak around behind my dad's back? I can't do that. Besides, maybe they're right. Maybe Benny and my dad are right. Too many distractions, and I can't focus. I don't want to let my team down. It was too close yesterday.

My eyes stare at the register. "Probably not until the season's over." I meet her eyes again. "I'm really sorry, Lauren."

Another customer comes through the front door. "Yeah," she says. "Me too." She looks past me and says hello to the person who's just walked in. That's my cue to leave.

I hold the bag up. "Thanks," I say. "I'll see you around."

"See ya later," she says, not even looking at me.

As I leave, I glance at a picture hanging on the wall. It says YOU CAN'T BUY HAPPINESS, BUT YOU CAN BUY DOUGHNUTS, AND THAT'S KIND OF THE SAME THING.

Man, I wish that were true. Because although I'm leaving with two doughnuts, I am not leaving happy, that's for sure.

61 Lauren

THERE'S ONE Chinese
restaurant in the entire
town of Willow.

Inside, the red booths
and tacky light fixtures
confirm what Stasia's
told me about the place.
A person looking for
authentic Chinese food
would be sorely disappointed.

Small-town America,
they say to know you
is to love you, but the
qualities you possess
kind of make me laugh.

Still, Stasia takes me
to Ming's after work
because she's crazy
in love with their egg rolls.

I tell her she's smart
to be crazy about
them instead of
a stupid boy because
egg rolls can't really
break your heart.

"Eating the last one is pretty sad," she says.

The thing is,
there's sad,
and then there's
feels-like-a-punch-in-the-gut sad.

I'm sad it's raining today.
I'm sad I can't afford the jeans I want.
I'm sad the egg rolls are gone.

or

I'm sad my mom made me leave.
I'm sad my brother isn't with me.
I'm sad it ended with Colby before it really began.

I'm so tired of
all the sadness,
I want to dump it
in the river and
watch it float away.

I glance over at a couple
who's been staring at me.
They quickly go back
to their plates of chow mein
and sweet and sour pork.

It's not the first time
I've felt eyes on me or
heard whispers about me,
and yet, tonight,
for some reason,
it gets to me.

I put my head in my hands
and sigh.

"We need to find a party," Stasia tells me.
"To cheer you up."

The Towne Pump is
our first stop, to see if
anyone's hanging around,
but the place is dead.

She texts a few people
but has no luck with
that, either.

We drive around,
listening to tunes,
trying to decide what

to do next, and the
town feels so small
in that moment, I feel
like I'm suffocating.

When we go past
the high school, Colby's
truck is in the parking lot,
and when I point it out,
she doesn't even ask.
She just stops.

It takes us a while,
but we finally
figure out what he's
doing there.

He didn't cancel
because
he wanted to.

He canceled
because
he had to.

I don't know
who I feel more
sorry for,
me or him.

62 Colby

SUNDAY AFTERNOON, I head to the hospital. When I ask if Benjamin Lewis can have visitors, I'm thrilled that the lady tells me he can, and directs me to his room.

I take the elevator to the fourth floor and am walking down the hall, toward room 412, when his mom steps out.

She pulls me into a hug when I reach her. "So good to see you, Colby. Before you go in there, let's talk for a minute."

We walk out to the small waiting area.

"How's he doing?" I ask as we sit down.

"He's talking some, which is great. They say that will improve every day now. But he has a lot of work to do."

"Work? Like what?"

She lets out a long breath. "He's going to have to relearn most everything — how to walk, how to brush his teeth, how to put his pants on. You know, everything we do without thinking about it and take for granted."

I look down at my lap and close my eyes. She can't be saying this. I don't want her to be saying this. I don't know what I was expecting. A miracle, maybe.

She continues. "Soon we'll have to move him to a rehabilitation center. We're trying to decide what to do. The best one in the country is all the way in Atlanta, Georgia. Insurance would pay for most of it, but one of us would have to take time off from work so we could go with him. And living apart, with only one income, I'm just not sure we can do it."

I look up. "I had no idea. I thought he'd go home with you. I guess I didn't know . . . how bad it really is."

She pats my arm. "I know. I wish he could go home too. But no." She looks at me, tears welling up. "He might not seem like the same Benny, but he's in there. Don't worry if he doesn't say much to you, okay?"

"Okay."

"Russ can hardly stand to see him like this. He's only been by once since he woke up. He's pretty upset about the whole thing. I guess what I'm trying to say is, I know it's hard. But it's important for him to know we're behind him." She sits up straight and blinks a few times before she smiles. "I'm so glad you're here. Are you ready?"

"Yeah. I'm ready."

When I walk into the room, there are cards and flowers spread out everywhere. Benny's in his bed, watching television. He's wearing a knit hat, with a big bandage around his head that the hat doesn't fully cover. Mr. Lewis gets up from the chair he's sitting in and shakes my hand. "Thanks for coming, Colby. I know Benny's glad to see you."

"Not as glad as I am to see him," I say.

He sits back down, and I turn to Benny. "Hey, man. How's it going?"

"Okay," he says slowly. Methodically.

I look at Mrs. Lewis, suddenly aware of how awkward this is. What am I supposed to say? Does he want to hear about the team, or will that make things worse? The last thing I want to do is depress him because he's in here and I'm out there, playing the game he loves more than anything else in the world.

"Don't you just love all of these cards and flowers?" she asks. "Every day, more and more come. Letters too. All kinds of letters, telling him to stay strong and that people are praying for him."

"Yep," Mr. Lewis chimes in. "Some people even send money, if you can believe that. There's some mighty fine people in this world, that's for sure."

I go over to the bed and look at my friend. He looks at me.

"One of the finest, right here," I say. I grab a chair and pull it up to the side of Benny's bed. "So, you wanna hear about Friday's game?" I ask him.

"Is . . . the Hulk . . . green?"

I laugh. Tears fill my eyes, both happy and sad ones. Benny's mom is right. He's in there. "That would be a yes."

And so, I start in. I tell him about the game, leaving out the part about how I messed up so much because I couldn't stop thinking about him not being able to play.

He has a lot of work to do.

"We won the game for you," I tell him after I've given him the quarter-by-quarter rundown. "We can't wait until you're back out there with us."

The look in his eyes tells me he's not so sure about that. I know the chances are slim to none, but doesn't he need something to work toward? Something to fight for?

I stand up, grip his hand, and hold it firm. "I believe," I say. Because the thing is, when it comes to Benny, I do.

If anyone can come back from this and make a full recovery, it's him. He's strong. He's tough. And he's got a team of believers behind him, and we will not let him forget who he is and where he comes from. He can do it. I know he can.

"You know the rule," I tell him. "You gotta say it."

It comes out softly. Hesitantly. "I . . . believe."

I sit back down, glancing at his mom and dad as I do. They're both smiling. "Awesome. That's a good starting place, right there. Coach would be proud, Benny."

The corners of his mouth turn up just slightly.

"Yep. He'd be proud."

63 Lauren

Dear Colby,
I need to talk to you. Will you meet
me at lunch? On the football bleachers?
Please. It's important.
Lauren

64 | Colby

I TELL myself I won't go. Because that's the easiest thing to do.

I read the note Monday morning, after Stasia passes it to me in the hallway like we're fourth graders. I crumple it up, toss it into my locker, and tell myself to forget about it. Whatever she has to say, it won't change anything.

But as the day goes on, and lunchtime draws closer and closer, my resolve softens. And when the bell rings, and kids stream toward the cafeteria, I realize there's no way I'll be able to stay away.

First of all, I'm curious. And second of all, I like her. Damn it — I *really* like her.

It's gray and cloudy, but no rain. I head toward the field and see Lauren walking a ways ahead of me. At least I think it's Lauren; she's got the hood up on her pink sweatshirt, like she wants to be incognito for this meeting.

I almost turn around and go back inside. No, I tell myself, I need to face her. Get it over with.

I follow her through the parking lot and onto the field. She starts climbing the bleachers, and I watch as she goes all the way to the top.

When she finally turns and sits down, dropping her back-pack beside her, I wave and then take the stairs up, slowly. I went for a long run yesterday, after talking to Benny, hoping it'd clear my head. My body probably could have used a day of rest, now that I think about it.

"You look like you're in pain," she says when I reach her.

I stand there, looking down at her. Her eyes are warm. Kind. She seems concerned. "Nah. I'm okay." I push her backpack down to the step below and take a seat.

She unzips one of the pockets on her bag and pulls out a sandwich. "You want half? It's turkey and cheese."

"No. You eat it. I'll grab something from a machine on my way to class."

"You can't have lunch out of a vending machine," she says.

I smile. "Says the girl who practically lives on Bugles."

She tries to hand me the sandwich. "But you're an athlete. You need real food." My hands stay in my lap. She raises her eyebrows and asks in the sweetest voice, "Please?"

I take it and say thanks. While I inhale my half in about three bites, she gets a bottle of water and two apples out of her bag.

"Wow," I say, picking up the water. "You thought of everything. It's like a picnic or something."

She hands me one of the apples and sets the other one in her lap. "I really wanted to talk to you and figured lunch would be the best time."

I stare at the apple because it's easier that way. "Look, Lauren, I know I said it before, but I really am sorry. About Saturday. It's just —"

"Please don't. Colby, I know. I know what happened. Saturday night, Stasia and I were driving by here, and we saw your truck. So we got out. We saw you and your dad on the field. At least, I assume it was your dad?"

I look up at the sky and exhale slowly. Suddenly it feels like I've swallowed a brick. How can I possibly explain how obsessed my dad is when it comes to football and me?

Her hand gently squeezes my arm. "Hey. Please don't be embarrassed. It's okay. I understand weird parents. Trust me."

I look at her. "Yeah. It was my dad. He wasn't happy about how I played Friday."

"That's why you canceled?"

"Yeah. He says I've got enough on my plate. I need to stay focused."

We sit there in silence for a while, while she eats her sandwich. I take a few bites of the apple.

It's getting more and more awkward by the second. Why did she ask me here? What else does she want me to say?

65 : Lauren

THERE ARE a million things
I want to say.

I've liked you since I met you.

I'm pretty sure
you have no idea how
much I like you.

I don't think I even knew myself
until Saturday, when my
hopes of spending more time with you
flew out the window as you left.

Maybe I've fallen too fast.
Maybe I should just let you go.
Maybe I'm stupid, sitting here,
trying to find the words to
tell you what you mean to me.

That day, when you handed me
my key, it was like fate stepped in
and said, "You two need to meet."

I think fate got it right.
I don't want us to get it wrong.

Who knows what's
going to happen
next week or
next month?
All I know is, I don't
want weeks or months
to go by without
talking to you again.

These are all the things
I wish I could tell you.

Instead, what comes out is,
"Can we at least be friends?"

66 | Colby

"FRIENDS?"

"Yeah," she says as she stuffs the empty sandwich bag into her backpack. "I mean, with Benny in the hospital, you could probably use a good friend. Right?"

I hand her the water bottle. As she takes a drink, I think about that. Friends. With a girl. Nothing else.

"Do you think that's possible?" I ask.

She nods. "Absolutely."

"Really?"

"Of course," she says confidently.

"I don't think I've been friends with a girl since, like, second grade. This girl, Vy, lived across the street from me, and we'd run through the sprinkler together in the summer. And eat Popsicles. And play with potato bugs."

"Oh, yeah. I love potato bugs. The way you pick them up and they roll into a ball? So awesome."

"Yeah."

She looks at me. "So, is that a yes?"

I shrug. "Sure. Why not? Benny'd probably give me hell for it, but whatever. I guess he doesn't have to know. For now."

"How's he doing, anyway?" she asks, like a friend does.

"Okay, I guess. I saw him yesterday. Sometime soon, they're going to move him to a rehabilitation center. The one they want to get him into is in Atlanta, but it's going to take a lot to make that happen. Financially, I mean. I wish there was something I could do to help them."

"Then let's help him," she says. "You and me. We could do a fund-raiser, right? I bet people here at school would get behind it. I think everybody's dying to do something to help, they just don't know how."

"What kind of fund-raiser? Like a car wash or going door-to-door . . . ?"

Her eyes are big and bright. "I know. We'll have a gigantic bake sale. Like, the biggest bake sale ever. I can ask Mr. Curtiss to donate some doughnuts from the shop. And we could make stuff, and ask a bunch of other people to make stuff."

I hold my hands up. "Whoa, hold on. The only thing I've ever baked was an angel food cake where all we had to do was add water to the mix. I don't think you want me making something I'd probably have to pay people to eat."

She shakes her head. "Colby Pynes, are you serious? You've never baked cupcakes or chocolate chip cookies or brownies?"

I shrug. "No."

"That is so sad."

"Well, when you don't have a mom around most of your life . . . But you know, I could ask my grandma to make something. And I can help you with other stuff. Advertising. Setting up. Whatever."

"We'll need to do all of that, of course, but we *will* make something. It'll be more fun than playing with potato bugs, I promise."

"Wait, I know," I say. "We could put potato bugs *in* whatever we're making. Now *that* would be fun."

173

She wrinkles her nose. "Gross. You're such a . . . boy."

I hold my hands up. "Hey, you're the one who wanted to be friends with me, remember?"

"I remember," she says as she grabs a notebook and a pen from her backpack, opens it up, and starts writing.

"What are you doing?" I ask.

"Making a list. We have a lot to do." She looks up and must see panic in my eyes. "Don't worry. Football comes first for you. I get it."

"Just so you know," I say as I look down at the field, "I wish it didn't."

I gotta admit, she is pretty easy to talk to.

Now if she wasn't so easy to look at, this being friends thing would be a piece of cake.

MONDAY NIGHT,
I sit on the patio,
listening for the owl.

The clouds have
cleared, and so I
look at the stars
and think about
lunch on the bleachers.

Colby has
no mom,
and a dad
who doesn't see
his son for the person
he really is.

I have
no dad,
and a mom
who doesn't see
her daughter for the person
she really is.

We are different
and yet
we are
the same.

Like two stars
hanging out in the sky,
wanting so much
to be noticed,
to be part
of a constellation.

Maybe we will
become our
own constellation,
just the two of us.

Two stars,
side by side —
a pair of eyes
in the sky.

Together,
we see.
Together,
we dream.
Together,
we shine.

68 : Colby

SHE THINKS we can do it. Be friends.

Maybe we can. I'm thinking it's not going to be easy, but I didn't want to say no. I mean, it seems like something is better than nothing.

And she's right. I could use a friend right about now. Lately, my teammates don't seem to know how to be around me off the field. It's like Benny is there, between us, and they're afraid of doing or saying the wrong thing.

With Lauren, I feel comfortable. I think she knows there are two versions of me: the real me and the one everyone thinks is me.

And she doesn't care.

For whatever reason, she understands.

69 : Lauren

TUESDAY

"Hi, Lauren."

"Hi."

"How are you?"

"I'm all right. Busy."

"Oh? What's going on?"

"I'm organizing a big bake sale to help raise money for Benny and his family."

She smiles. "That's wonderful. When is it?"

"A week from Saturday. I have a flyer, if you're interested." I reach into my backpack and pull one out. She gets up from her chair and takes it from me.

"I'll definitely try to stop by," she says as she looks it over.

"That'd be great. Thanks."

"Are you going to bake something?"

"Yeah. Not sure what."

"Did you and your mom ever bake things together?"

I give a little grunt of indignation. I would have liked to, but I don't say that. There was one time, in fourth grade, when the school had a bake sale to raise money for new instruments for the music room. I asked my mom if we could make something, and she said no. She didn't have time. She said that a lot. She did give me a few dollars so I could buy some-thing at the sale, though. I bought cupcakes and shared them with my babysitter, Mrs. Neely.

"No," I tell her. "My mom wasn't really the baking type. My aunt Erica bakes a lot, though."

"How's it going, living with them? Everything all right?"

"Yes. They're great. I just wish they'd trust me."

"What do you mean?"

"I heard them talking one day. They don't trust me to watch my cousins. After what happened. Or, well, what sup-posedly happened."

"Hmm. Well, give it time."

"I know. It's okay. They're good people, I know that. And I can't really blame them, I guess."

"You know, Lauren, I'd love to hear your side of the story. You've been so close to telling me a couple of times and then you stop. How come?"

I stare at the window. "I don't know."

It's true. I don't. At first, it was because I didn't think it would do any good. Like, what's the point, rehashing it all? But now, if she thinks it might help, how do I know for sure that it won't?

"Are you afraid? Whatever you tell me is between us. You are safe here."

I stare at the tree outside the window. I wish I were there, hidden in the branches, the sky waiting for me. I imagine what that feels like — to open your wings and let the wind take you up and away.

It must take a lot of trust.

I take a deep breath. "It was late. The baby, my half brother, wouldn't stop crying. I thought he was sick. He felt warm, like he had a fever. I kept telling her we needed to get some infant Tylenol to help him feel better."

"By 'her,' you mean, your mom?" she asks.

"Right. She said Matthew would be fine, if she could just get him to sleep. But she was drinking that night, and the more he cried, the angrier she got. She started shaking him and shaking him, yelling at him to stop."

I look at Dr. Springer. "I was so scared. I'd never been as scared as I was that night. I tried to take him from her, but she wouldn't let me. She locked herself in her bedroom with him. I really thought she was going to hurt him." I gulp. "So I called 911 and asked them to send the police, because a baby was in danger. I gave our address, and then I hung up.

"When the police came, I was in the bathroom, throwing up, because I was so upset. So . . . afraid. My mom came into the bathroom when they started knocking. She started yelling at me, 'What have you done? Don't you know they'll take him from me? Is that what you want? Do you want to go to foster care? Because it won't just be him. It'll be you too.'"

I lower my head, the memory so strong, I swear the air suddenly smells like the liquor that was on her breath. "I shouldn't have called."

"Lauren, you did the right thing."

I shake my head. "I told her I'd fix it. I apologized and told her not to worry; I was going to fix it. So we went out there, and she held the baby, and one of the officers asked who called. I told him my mom was the one who called, because the baby had been crying and I got sick of it and started shaking him, and I wouldn't give him to her. I told them I was sorry, I knew it was wrong, and I promised them it would never happen again."

"So, you lied. To protect your mom."

My eyes fill with tears. "Yes. And then . . ."

"It's okay. Go on. What happened next?"

I bite my lip, tears streaming down my face now. I sniffle. "When the officer asked if my mom wanted to press charges, she said no, she just wanted me to get the message loud and clear that my behavior was unacceptable. After one of the officers gave me a stern talking-to, they left."

"But that's not the end of the story," she says.

I shake my head again. "My mom said we needed a break. Me and her. Some time apart. She thought I could stay with my grandma for a while, but my grandma said no. So she called my uncle Josh. And they agreed to take me in. I didn't fight her on it. In fact, I was as sweet as ever." I look down at my hands. "I kept hoping she'd change her mind. I can't believe I thought she'd change her mind."

The tears won't stop, but I don't feel embarrassed. I just feel so . . . sad.

Dr. Springer walks over to me with the box of tissues. I pull out a bunch and try to wipe the sadness away. Instead, I just smear it around.

"Thank you for telling me," she says as she sits back down. "I can see why that wouldn't be easy to share. And why you're having such terrible nightmares about your brother."

I jerk my head in her direction. "Why?"

"Because you're worried about him." She makes a note in her file. "I think I'd like to have a social worker go and check on him. Would that be all right? Your mother doesn't have to know the visit came about because of you."

"She won't hurt him," I say quickly. "I promise she won't." It's like I'm pleading with her to believe me. "It was just that one time, you know? Because she drank too much."

"Do you think your brother is better off with your mother than somewhere else?" she asks.

"Yes. Maybe. I . . . I don't know. Look, I know she wasn't the best mom, and that growing up, I wished for her to be different in some ways. But she never hurt me. I have to believe he's okay."

"I know you do," she says. "But I think checking on him is a good idea."

The truth is, I'm afraid my mom will know. She'll know it's because of me that they're checking. And then what?

Suddenly, there are too many scenarios playing out in my head. Did I make things better or worse by telling her the truth about what happened?

Something tells me I'm going to find out.

Part 3

....

"I want to sing like the birds sing, not worrying
about who hears or what they think."

— RUMI

70 | Colby

LAUREN AND her aunt Erica pulled things together quickly for the fund-raiser. They made flyers and put them all over town. An email chain was initiated, asking for donations to be dropped off early Saturday morning. The weekly newspaper agreed to put something on the front page about the event. And the best part is, the city is allowing us to use the big parking lot in the middle of downtown, where the Saturday Market is held in the summertime. A rental company is donating tables and canopies, so it'll look super nice and there will be plenty of space for the food.

I've been back to see Benny a few more times, and his mom is so thankful that we're doing this for them. I keep telling Lauren we aren't going to raise a million dollars selling cupcakes and maybe we should have thought of something else. And she keeps telling me you never know what might happen. For a girl who hasn't exactly had an easy time of it, she sure has a good attitude. Maybe some of it will rub off on me.

It's Friday night, after the game, and I'm in her aunt and uncle's kitchen, baking pies with Lauren. I imagine heaven smells like this kitchen right now.

As she carefully puts the crust on the top of a berry pie, I ask her, "You know, maybe we should have picked something easier to make."

"Like what? Rice Krispies Treats?"

"Right. What do those have, like, three ingredients?"

"You can't make good money on something like that. These pies will go for a lot."

"You really think so? How come?"

"Because pies are special. Pies say, 'I'm good and old-fashioned.'"

"Rather than, 'I'm cheap and easy'?"

She laughs. "Exactly! Who wants something cheap and easy?"

I raise my eyebrows. "About ninety percent of the football team?"

She pokes me with her elbow. "Stop it. You wait and see. These pies will fly off the tables tomorrow."

I look at the clock. I honestly don't know how much longer I can stay standing. "You mean today. It's after midnight. Are we going to be done anytime soon?"

"While this one bakes, we'll whip together a chocolate cream one, and then we're done." As she pinches the last of the crust, she studies my face. "You know what? I can do the last one by myself. You should go home."

"Are you sure?"

"I'm positive. See, it wouldn't be very helpful if you fell over from exhaustion and landed in the pies. Not helpful at all."

"Okay. Thanks. Do you want me to pick you up tomorrow and take you down there?"

She looks around at all the pies: nine so far. "Oh God. I didn't even think about logistics. How are we going to get all of these to the sale?"

"Easy. I'll put a sheet in the bed of my truck. We'll set them back there, and then fold the sheet over."

"A sheet?"

"Yeah. Why not? We'll tuck them in tight, I promise."

"You are so cute, you know that?" she says as she opens the oven door before she pops the pie inside. I want to tell her she's cuter, but I'm pretty sure that would be approaching flirting territory. That's a place we're both trying to stay far away from.

When she turns around, she says, "Okay. Your plan sounds good. I want to be there by eight. All the other volunteers are supposed to be there by eight thirty."

"I'll pick you up about fifteen minutes before eight, then."

We say good-bye and I let myself out. From the driveway, I can see her silhouette, no doubt starting in on the chocolate pie.

"You're cuter," I whisper into the cool night air. And then I get into my truck, glad I get to see her again in only eight short hours.

71 Lauren

LAST WEEK, Aunt Erica
asked me if I wanted
her help with the pies.

I told her I felt
like I wanted to try
and figure it out
on my own.

She gave me some
recipes and her tips
on how to make
a good, flaky crust
for the fruit pies.

She took me grocery
shopping to buy
all the ingredients.

And then she left
me alone, to do
the baking until
Colby came by later.

There is something
really soothing
about the act of baking.
Comforting.

It forces you to slow down.
To focus on the work.
To put everything else
out of your mind so you
can create something amazing
that wasn't there before.

I started with an easy one.
Two-minute Hawaiian Pie
with pudding, pineapple,
and coconut in a
graham-cracker crust.

One minute,
a lonely,
empty shell.

The next, with just the right mix
of ingredients and special care,
a sweet, sweet pie.

I think there is a lesson
to be learned there
somewhere.

72 Colby

WHEN I pull into the driveway and see that the lights are still on in the house, I curse my dad. I consider turning around and finding somewhere else to sleep so I don't have to walk in there and deal with him.

I'm so tired. I just want to go to bed. I don't want to talk about the game, what I did wrong, what I did right, how so much is on the line with every game I play.

Damn it. I just want to rest.

I get out and go inside. I tell myself the whole way I will not engage him. I will not let him talk to me right now. I will tell him I'm going to bed and I will mean it and I will do it.

I'm barely in the door, and he's right there, like mud on a pig, "Colby, what the hell? Where have you been?"

"There's a fund-raiser for Benny tomorrow, remember? I was helping a friend bake some pies."

"Well, I've been thinking all night about that play. In the second quarter? When you missed the pass. Colby, what happened? It was a good throw. You should have had it."

This is where I should walk away. This is where I should say, not now, I'm tired, I'm going to bed.

I look at him. He wants an answer. He wants to talk about this to death and know that I learned something from it so it won't happen again. Even though there's no guarantee of that, ever.

"I don't know, Dad. The throw was a little long, and I missed it. I'm sorry."

"We've talked about this before. You could have had it if you . . ."

He moves toward the kitchen table, and I follow him. We sit down. He keeps talking.

And I keep listening. Just like he wants me to.

73 : Lauren

I'M ABOUT to turn out the lights
and go to bed when Erica appears.

She surveys the kitchen and smiles.
"The pies look amazing. Great job."

"Colby helped. I hope they taste okay."
I look at her. "How come you're up?"

"Can't sleep. Crazy schedule does that to me.
I'm going to watch some TV. Something boring."

She looks like a little girl, in a T-shirt and
pajama pants, her hair sticking every which way.

I have a sudden urge to hug her.
Because I wonder if she knows.

Knows how much I appreciate everything they've done.
Knows how much I've come to love their family.

Knows I haven't been this happy in a long time.
Knows how much I want them to love and trust me.

"Do you want me to stay up with you?" I ask.
She smiles. "No. Go to bed. Big day tomorrow."

"Yeah. It is. Well, good night, then."
And as I walk past, I do it. I give her a hug.

She wraps her arms around me and says,
"Good night, honey. Sweet dreams."

As I start to head to my room, I say, "Thanks."
I hope she knows how very much I mean it.

74 : Colby

THE NEXT morning, when I step outside, the faint scent of burning wood in the cool autumn air, I see an old car parked on the street in front of our house. It looks familiar, and yet, I can't quite place it.

Russ steps out and waves. Of course. Now it comes together. It's been a while since I've seen him. Pretty sure the last time was at Mrs. Lewis's birthday party.

You'd never know Russ and Benny were brothers just by looking at them. Where Benny is all muscle, Russ is skin and bones. Soon as he was out of high school, he moved out, into a crappy little apartment with a couple of friends. He works at a grocery store. Started as a bag boy in high school, now he's a cashier. Benny used to say, "Now that's exactly what I *don't* want my life to look like."

"Hey, man," he says as we meet in the driveway. I throw the sheet I'm holding into the back of my truck and shake his hand.

"Hey, Russ. You're up kinda early, aren't you?"

"Yeah, I wanted to be sure to catch you. Look, I know the bake sale is going on today, and I want to see if I can do anything to help. I can't bake anything worth shit, but could I do something else?"

I stick my hands in my pockets. "That's great you want to help, but they're all set with volunteers. Besides, this is about us helping you guys. You don't need to do a thing."

He looks past me, toward my house. "I wish I could do more to help him. I cannot stand being in that hospital room, man. I know that's terrible, but I'm not good at pretending everything's fine when it's not, you know?"

"I don't think you have to pretend," I tell him. "Mostly I think it's good for Benny to know that we care about him. That we support him. Right?"

"I guess. I just want to do something. I mean, something that matters. That makes a difference."

I say it as nice as I can. "Russ, being there for him, talking to him, that matters. More than anything."

He sighs. "I want him to get better. I want him to be his old self."

"Well, that's what this bake sale's all about — helping him get into a good place where he can work toward that. Let's hope people open their wallets wide today, in the name of Benny and baked goods."

"Maybe I'll stop by and get him a cake or something," he says.

"That's a great idea. I bet he'd love that."

"You sure you don't need any help?" he asks as I pull the truck keys out of my pocket.

"I'm sure," I tell him. "But thanks for the offer."

"All right, then. I'll leave you to it. Thanks, Colby. For doing this for him."

"You're welcome."

As I drive to Lauren's, I think about Russ and realize if it's hard for me to imagine Benny never playing football again, it's gotta be even harder for his family. I think they all looked at him as the one with the real chance at greatness. And now it must feel like that chance is gone.

I want to believe there's always a chance, though. Isn't that what Coach has been trying to tell us with the cards and the signs and the pep talks? That believing is more important than anything. It's what keeps you going, even when things look bad.

And I know things look pretty bad right now.

But he's alive. He's out of the coma. He's talking.

And really, from here on out, things can only get better. Just how better, that's the question.

75 : Lauren

WITH PIES
in the back,
we head to
the spot
downtown
where we will
sell fabulous treats
and collect
donations.

Colby is quiet.

Are people
going to come?

Will it be
enough?

Are we doing
all we can?

They are questions
with answers

we don't have
quite yet.

I want to
reach over.
Hold his hand.
Tell him it
will be okay.

Would a friend
do that?

This whole
"being friends"
is hard.

Harder than
I thought.

There's a line
we're not supposed
to cross, except
the line is not
clear and not straight
and seems to move
at times.

Honestly,
I wish I could

just erase
the stupid line.

Build a bridge instead,
so there'd be nothing
to get in our way.

76 | Colby

LAUREN'S QUIET.

Is she nervous? Worried about the turnout? Or wondering if everything will go all right? I don't want her to worry.

"You know, this is a good thing you're doing. Benny's family appreciates it a lot."

"Thanks," she says. "It's been fun, working on this. I'm glad I've had something else to think about besides . . ." She stops. Smiles. "I think it's going to be a great day. I'm excited."

I wonder what she was going to say. I almost ask her but decide now's not the time. "Yeah. Me too. So which pie should I buy?"

She turns and looks at me. "Well, I think the question is, what do you like?"

I raise my eyebrows. "You mean, as far as a pie goes?"

As soon as I say it, I realize my mistake. I shouldn't have said that. But it's hard to stay away from flirting territory all the time. I mean, it's pretty fun there. Especially with Lauren.

I want her to reply with something like, "No, not as far as a pie goes, as far as a girl goes."

And then I would say something like, "Well, you should know better than anyone right now."

Then she would get all flustered and not know how to respond. And I could reach over for her hand, and take it in mine.

But Lauren, she's good. She keeps things right where they are supposed to be. She replies, "Of course, as far as pie goes. That's what we're talking about, right?"

"I guess I like berry or apple," I say, pretty unenthusiastically, because what I really want to say is, *I like* you.

"Well, you'll get first choice," she says.

I want to say, *I choose* you.

Clearly, this being friends thing has become a challenge for me. But that's okay. I thrive on challenges (or at least, this is what I tell myself).

When we get to the location of the bake sale, the tables and canopies are all set up and the place looks fantastic. Mr. Curtiss, Lauren's boss, is setting up a couple of cash registers with change, which he offered to do.

Lauren goes over to talk to him and I simply stand back and watch her for a minute. I could watch her all day, actually, but I have pies to carry over.

Very carefully, one at a time, I take the pies to a table. Lauren comes over a little while later with colorful doilies, the ingredients lists, and the price tags. Each of the pies made with pudding are in boxes with a couple of ice packs on the bottom. The other pies, she puts on little stands she made. When she's done, I have to say, the table looks amazing.

"I'm gonna buy the berry one and put it in my truck, if that's okay?" I tell her.

"Yeah. Absolutely. Mr. Curtiss can take your money."

"Do you have something set up for donations too?" I ask.

"He brought a couple of huge jars for that. They're perfect."

"Okay, good."

"The volunteers are starting to arrive," she says. "I should go give them their directions." She looks nervous as she bites her lip.

"You want me to go with you?"

She considers it for a moment. "Actually, could you hang around and help people carry stuff to the tables, if they need it?"

"Sure. I can do that." I pick up the berry pie, along with the ingredients list. "Let me buy this one first."

"Okay. Well, I guess I'll see you around."

She starts to leave when I call out, "I can give you a ride home later. If you want. Since, you know, you don't have your bike."

She turns around. Smiles. "You love rubbing that silly bike in my face, don't you?"

"No. No! I love your bike. It's a two-for-one, remember? Like this pie. It'll be delicious *and* it's for a good cause. I'm all about the two-for-ones, I promise."

"Like, you give me a ride home *and* you get my charming company for ten minutes?"

I nod. Maybe a little too enthusiastically. "Exactly!"

"Okay," she says. "You're on."

I practically skip as I make my way over to pay for the pie. Until I realize that after the bake sale today, we won't really have an excuse to hang out anymore.

I wonder if she's a good student? Maybe she could help me with some homework.

77 : Lauren

CUPCAKES
and fruit tarts.

Brownies
and scones.

Cookies
and lemon bars.

Éclairs
and pies.

Hundreds
of sweet treats.

All of them
sold.

Jars filled
with money.

Big bills
and checks.

An anonymous
donation

for ten thousand
bucks.

Joy and
gratitude.

Pats on
the back.

Small-town
living.

Not so bad
after all.

78 : Colby

HOLY DOUBLE chocolate brownies, Batman.

It's insane. How much money we raised. How many people came. How empty the tables are now that it's over.

Benny's family stopped by and were blown away by what they saw. It felt like the whole town came out to buy baked goods and donate money. Russ bought a big triple-layer chocolate fudge cake and said they'd take it to Benny to celebrate. He was moved to a rehab center in Lansford last week, but Mrs. Lewis said this extra money will allow her to take a leave of absence so they can go to Atlanta for at least a couple of months.

I'm thankful he'll be going. And yet, when I think of him getting on that plane and leaving here for an unknown length of time, it hurts like hell.

I want him to go.

But, God, I don't want him to go.

Lauren's aunt and uncle volunteer to get the money in order and take it to the bank so they can give Benny's family a big, fat check.

When Lauren gets in my truck, she leans back in the seat, closes her eyes, and says, "Wow."

"Yeah," I concur.

She rolls her head toward me and opens her eyes. "It was awesome, huh? I'm so proud of us."

"Me too."

"Maybe now people will stop thinking the worst about me," she says. "About why I'm here, you know?"

"I'm sure they will but try not to worry about what people think." I swallow hard, trying to get the nerve to do what I want to do next. "Do you, um, have to get home right away? I thought maybe we could make a stop first."

She shrugs. "Okay. Can I borrow your phone and let my aunt know?"

While she calls, I drive. The clouds have cleared, and it's pretty nice out. Now that it's October, I know it won't be like this much longer. I look over at Lauren, and I think, *in more ways than one.*

I want to make the most of this. Whatever "this" is.

I pull into the Safeway parking lot. She raises her eyebrows. Before she has time to say anything, I tell her, "I need to run in and get something. You stay here. I'll be right back."

I hustle through the store, grabbing what I need, and make it back to the truck in record time.

"Well, that was fun," she teases. "Probably didn't need to call my aunt and tell her I'd be late for a stop at Safeway."

I start up the truck. "Okay, if you want to get technical, we're making two stops. That was the first one. Now on to the second one."

She looks at the grocery bag sitting between us. "Can I take a peek?"

"No!" I grab the bag and pull it close to me. "You'll find out soon enough, since we'll be there in about two minutes." I look at her. "Patience, grasshopper. It's a small town, remember?"

"How could I forget, after I just met almost everyone who lives here at the bake sale? I still can't believe how many people showed up."

I look at her after I pull out onto the road. "Yeah, you just witnessed the best of small-town life. We come together and pull for our own, that's for sure."

"It's really great," she says, staring out the window. "It felt good to be a part of something so important. Even if it wasn't for very long."

"That's why people love football, you know. Why they love coming out to the games and supporting our team."

She looks at me. Gives my leg a little shove. "But football isn't *that* important."

"Maybe not to you. But to a lot of people, it is."

"Why? I don't get it."

I shrug. "I have a few different theories. Mostly, I think it's because for a little while every week, folks are able to forget about their dull lives. They have something to believe in. Something to hope for. And it feels good to believe and hope."

"But, Colby, it's just a *game*. Why don't they find something in their own lives to believe in and hope for?"

I smile. "*Because* it's just a game. Putting your hopes on something like a football team rather than yourself is so much easier, right? And if things don't go the way you want, well, there's always next year. Always another chance to try again. To hope again. But in life? Sometimes we only get one chance."

She doesn't say anything after that.

Not a thing.

And I wonder what that means.

79 Lauren

I KNOW all about
that thing
called hope.

Except lately,
hope and I
get along
about as well
as hawks and mice.

Sometimes
I find myself hoping
my mom will call me
and ask me to come home.

Other times
I'm hoping
I can just stay here,
with a family
I've grown to love.

My hopes change
along with my moods,

depending on what
I choose to remember
on any given day.

Maybe what I hope for
most of all
is that everything
simply works out
for the best,
even if I don't know
exactly what that looks like.

Colby's right.
It'd be a lot easier
to put my hopes
on a football team.

80 Colby

WHEN I pull into the parking lot of Queen Elizabeth Elementary School, Lauren gives me a funny look.

"This is where Benny and I met," I explain as I park the truck. I notice the front doors are still a bright yet inviting blue, like they've always been. I turn the engine off. "He moved here in the third grade. At lunchtime, he sat down next to me. I watched as he ate his hamburger and Tater Tots in about fifteen seconds flat." I laugh. "Man, that guy *still* loves Tater Tots. Anyway, when he was done, he turned and looked at me. And I'll never forget what happened next."

"What?" Lauren asks. I love how truly interested she is in this story.

"Benny said, 'This is my favorite part of school.' And then I said, 'You mean eating lunch?' And he said, 'Nah. After we eat. Going to recess. Playing with friends.' And I said, without thinking, because I was a stupid eight-year-old boy, 'But you're new. You don't have any friends.' He looked at me with those big brown eyes and said, 'Maybe not yet. But I will. You'll see. Now hurry up and eat so we can go play.'"

I swallow hard. I remember the moment so clearly, it's like it happened an hour ago. "And he was right. By the end of recess, we were friends. But you know what's really amazing to me? He could have sat anywhere that day. But it's like God knew, and he sat him next to me."

"Knew what?" she asks.

"Knew we needed each other."

It hangs in the air for a second, and I want to say, I still need him. Benny. My best friend. And that I miss him like crazy.

But I don't need to say it. She knows. How can she not know?

I quickly open my door. "Come on. We're gonna go have a pie picnic. On the playground."

She smiles. "A pie picnic! Awesome."

I grab the sheet and the pie while Lauren carries the grocery bag. We walk around to the back of the school and stand there, scanning the place for a good place to sit.

"Over here," she says. I follow her like she asked, all the way to the top of the play structure.

I point to a steering wheel that juts out from one side. "Who's gonna fly the spaceship? Or whatever this is we're on."

"Don't worry," Lauren says as she takes the sheet tucked under my arm and spreads it out. "The driver's there; you just can't see him. We're in good hands."

"Oh. Right. An invisible driver. I forgot that's a possibility on playground spaceships. What's his name?"

She opens the bag and takes out the paper plates and plastic silverware I bought at the store. "Uh, how about Rain Man? After all, he's an excellent driver."

"Rain Man?"

"Yeah. You've never seen that movie?"

I take a seat on the sheet and set the pie down in the middle. "No. I haven't. What's it about?"

Lauren sits across from me. "Two brothers who didn't know each other existed until their father died. One of them is autistic with lots of quirks. The other is kind of a selfish jerk. They go on a road trip together, and the asshole brother becomes less so, and really comes to love his quirky brother." She picks up a knife and starts slicing the pie. "In the end, these two people, who were pretty lonely before they met, end up with something they didn't even know they were missing." She looks at me. "It's sweet, right? It won a bunch of Oscars. It's one of my mom's favorites."

I nod. "I'll have to check it out. You know, you haven't said much about your mom. If you want to talk about her, about what happened or whatever, I hope you know you can."

She puts a piece of pie on a plate and passes it to me. "Thanks, but there isn't a whole lot to say."

I fish a fork out of the box of utensils. "Do you miss her?"

Another piece of pie goes on a plate. "Not really," she says too quickly. Her eyes float up to meet mine. "Well . . . maybe once in a while."

I'm not sure what to say to that. If she isn't ready to tell me more, I don't want to push her. I simply say, "Yeah. I get that. It sneaks up on you sometimes. The missing, I mean."

She's pushing her pie around on her plate with her fork, and I want so much to lean over and take her face in my hands so I can kiss her. Make her feel better. Because whatever happened, I can tell she's hurting. Maybe she doesn't want to admit it, maybe she doesn't want to talk about it, and yeah, maybe she wants to forget it ever happened, whatever "it" is. But I see it in her eyes — she's having a hard time.

"You know, Benny said something to me recently," I tell her. "He said we gotta take the bad stuff with the good. That it's just how life is. If you think about it, no one has it good all the time. You don't, I don't, Benny certainly doesn't. So maybe we have to just hold on and believe that eventually good stuff will come out of the bad stuff. Somehow. Some way."

She tilts her head just a little. Her eyes narrow. It's like she's studying me. "Do you think something good will come out of Benny getting hurt?"

I think of all the people, an entire town, coming together to help one guy.

I think of Lauren and me, sitting here, talking and eating pie together.

I think of Benny. Everything he's been through. His unknown future.

"If I want to get out of bed every morning, I *have* to believe something good will come of it."

I pick up my plate and take a bite of the pie Lauren and I made together last night.

"And who knows," I add. "Maybe something already has."

I IMAGINE Rain Man
standing at the wheel,
taking us up,
higher and higher.

We travel,
through stardust
and moonbeams,
to a galaxy
all our own.

A million miles
away from here.

From the land
of regrets and
of missing
and of longing to fit in.

We'll belong
to the universe,
and the universe
will belong to us.

It's a long way
to go.

I wonder,
how far
do you have to go
to really leave
the past

behind?

82 | Colby

"I WISH it'd been me," I tell her.

Her head shoots up, like a rocket, eyes glaring at me. "Don't say that."

"It's true, though. Football might have been Benny's ticket to college. I know I'm supposed to think positive. I'm supposed to believe that he can come out of this better and stronger than before. And I'm trying, Lauren. I'm really trying. But if it'd been me, I wouldn't miss football that much." I swallow. "But with Benny, it's, like, all he thinks about."

She sets her pie down and gets to her feet. She goes to the railing and stands there, looking out toward the soccer field. "You just said you have to believe something good will come out of it. Maybe something will. For Benny, I mean. We don't know. Maybe he'll meet the girl of his dreams down in Atlanta. Maybe someday he'll get married and have beautiful babies. Maybe he'll become a politician. A good one, you know? One who works to make the world a better place." She turns her head toward me. "You don't know what comes next. No one knows, really, but anything's possible. Isn't it?"

The way she's fighting for him, fighting for his happiness, when she's never even met the guy, makes my heart feel like it's just doubled in size. I stand up and go over to where she's standing. I lean on the railing and look out at the playground.

"Benny and me," I say. "We'd run around out there, chasing balls or chasing girls or, half the time, chasing each other. Since high school, it feels like all we've done is chase that damn championship football title."

"That's a lot of chasing," she says.

"And here I am, feeling like I should be chasing something and instead all I'm doing is running away from everything." I shake my head. "Is that messed up or what?"

She touches my arm. I can feel her looking at me. "So stop running. Just stand still for a while, and see what happens."

I rise, straight and tall, and turn so I'm facing Lauren. She's right there. I could take her in my arms. I could lean down and kiss her. I could stop running away from my feelings, from my father, from Benny even.

I could.

But I don't.

Not so much because of my dad or the team or any of that, but because Lauren and I made an agreement. I don't want to mess this up. How comfortable we are. How easy it is. And maybe, right now, I need a friend more than I need anything else. Who knows — with everything she's not telling me, maybe she does too.

So I quickly turn and point at our abandoned plates. "Hey, check it out. You've hardly eaten any of our pie. Are you trying to tell me something? Does it suck? God, did we sell a bunch of awful pies to people? They're going to hate us."

"They're not going to hate us."

I reach down, pick up her plate and fork, and hand it to her. She takes a bite. "It's really good, you know," she says.

"I'm curious. Do you still like bake sales after all that work?"

"Yep." She smiles. "Maybe even more than I did before."

I could say the same thing about my feelings for Lauren. Instead, I eat my pie.

83 : Lauren

AS WE'RE preparing to leave,
six or seven crows
fly in and land in a tree
across the field.

They are beautiful
and spooky
all at the same time.

"A murder of crows," I tell Colby.
"Some view the appearance
of them as an omen of death."

They sit in the tree, cawing.

"Not the death of a person," he says.
"Let's say the death of . . ."

"Despair," I reply.

"Yeah," he says.
"And fear."

I start to ask
what he's afraid of,
exactly.

But ironically,
I'm afraid
to ask.

84 | Colby

WHEN I get home, Gram and Grandpa are watching the news.

"You just missed it," Gram says. "They had a short piece on your bake sale today."

"It sounds like it was a huge success," Grandpa says. "Sure were a lot of people there when we stopped by."

I take a seat on the sofa, suddenly realizing how tired I feel. "Yeah, it went really well. Thanks for coming."

Gram smiles. "Our pleasure. Your dad was there too. Did you see him?"

"Yeah, I did. He said he made a nice-size donation."

"So Benny will go to Atlanta, then?" Gram asks.

I swallow hard. "Yeah. Not sure when. Soon, I guess."

Gram stands up. "I'll get dinner ready." She looks at me. "I'm proud of you, Colby. We all are. This has been a difficult time, and you've really shown the community what a fine young man you are."

"We're going to have pie to celebrate, right, Judith?" Grandpa says.

Gram smiles. "You bet. I bought a beautiful berry pie for us to have tonight. Doesn't that sound good?"

Of all the things she could have bought. It makes me laugh. "Sounds great."

85 : Lauren

AT HOME,
there is pizza
and bowls of Bugles
and sparkling cider
and cake.

Three cakes, actually.

"I couldn't resist," Erica says
when I see them and laugh.

Uncle Josh
pours the cider
into champagne flutes.

Little hands hold
fancy glasses, and
their eyes are big
and bright, as if they've
been given magic
to sip on.

"To Lauren," Josh says.
"You did an amazing thing today."

"To Lauren," Erica says.

Clink,
clink,
clink.
The sound of our glasses.

Love,
love,
love.
The sound of my heart.

86 | Colby

AFTER DINNER, I grab the laptop and go to my room.

I've got emails from the teams trying to recruit me, but I delete them, unread.

Coach has sent me a link, with a note:

> I know I've told you boys to stay away from news
> articles and the like. That it doesn't do you any good to
> be reading about what others think about you, because
> the most important thing is what you think of yourself.
> I truly believe that worrying about what other people
> think will only mess with your head in the worst
> possible way. But I'm making an exception this one
> time. This article is one you should read. Great game
> last night, Pynes. Keep it up! Coach Sperry

I click on the link. And then I start reading.
The name of the article is "The Power of Believing."

> *When I woke up yesterday morning and saw the*
> *weather report, my first thought was, "It'll be a good*
> *night for some high school football." But it was my*
> *second thought that surprised me: "You should go watch*
> *the Willow High Eagles play." Why did it surprise me?*

Because it's a two-hour drive from where I live, and I have my pick of at least a dozen games here in the Greater Portland area on any given Friday night during football season.

But I'd read about the accident that almost killed their guard Benjamin Lewis. And I'd read about how the team keeps fighting, week after week, to keep their playoff dreams alive. And I'd read specifically about Lewis's best friend, Colby Pynes, and his struggle on and off the field to keep going without his friend by his side.

Something pulled me to Willow last night, and while the thought initially surprised me, I've learned to follow those callings. They usually happen for a reason, and I'm often rewarded in ways I don't expect. And so it was as I found myself sitting in the bleachers at the Willow Eagles football field.

The story here is not the game, which was good, but not spectacular. The Eagles beat the Panthers, 24–17. The Eagles clearly have talent. They also have drive and ambition, and anyone watching them knows they work hard.

But it was the two words they said before they took the field that caught my attention. "I believe," they yelled.

I turned to the person sitting next to me and asked what it was all about. The older gentleman smiled and said, "It's the team's motto. They carry around cards that say I BELIEVE. It's on a sign in their locker room. And they say it before every game."

"Are you related to one of the players?" I asked him.

He told me he was. He was Colby Pynes's grandfather. We talked about the accident involving his best friend and how Pynes has spent every spare minute at the hospital in the weeks that have followed. "But he never let his team down," Mr. Pynes told me. "He didn't let anyone down."

As I sat there, I tried to imagine what that must be like. To have your best friend and teammate suddenly ripped away from you, in the blink of an eye. I wondered where you find the strength to keep going, at the ripe young age of seventeen.

I had one more question for Mr. Pynes. "Do you think those two words have helped him through this? I mean, does he truly believe?"

When Mr. Pynes looked at me this time, he had tears in his eyes. He said, "Yes. I think Colby's learned that the most important thing is to keep the faith. To believe the impossible can become possible. Every time the Eagles win a game this season, it's against all odds, really. Hearts are broken, and anyone who has tried to play a sport, all in, with a broken heart, knows how hard it is. But that's the thing. Every time this team wins a game, they're reminded that anything is possible. And they realize it applies to their friend and teammate, Benny Lewis, as well. With each game, the belief grows even stronger."

At that point, I told Mr. Pynes who I was and got his permission to quote him. On the two-hour drive home, I thought about what he'd said. And I thought about what I had witnessed on and off the field.

I've come to the conclusion that I saw a power last night that cannot really be described in words. The power of believing. But more than that, the power of love, for a teammate and a friend. When you combine the two, well, I'll just say it — anything is possible. And I fully expect to see the Willow High Eagles playing in the state championship game.

I left that game last night a believer. One hundred percent.

LATER,
when I'm in bed,
Erica comes in.

I'm reading a book
about a girl who
learns her mother
was once
a mermaid.

Erica sits down.
Smiles.
One of those
I'm-trying-to-look-
happy-but-I'm-really-not
kind of smiles.

Something's up.
I know it.
There's bad news.
Everything's been
going so well,

and it feels like
right now,
in this moment,
everything is
about to change.

"Your mom called earlier today.
While you were out."

I don't say anything.
I know there's more.

"I told her you're doing really well.
Then I asked if maybe she'd like
to come down and see you.
I told her that she and Matthew
are welcome to stay here."

I run my fingers
back and forth
across the smooth
and shiny book cover,
staring at it.

Maybe if I stare at it
long enough, I can
become the girl in the story.
The girl who has
a mermaid for a mother.

Her mother is beautiful
and loves the sea,
but she loves her family more.

More than anything
else in the world.

She is kind and
caring and chooses her
children above all else.

"Lauren, she's moving.
She's going to North Carolina."

My head snaps up.

"North Carolina?
That's so far.
Why there?"

"She didn't say.
She simply said she needs a change.
In a month or two, she'll be going."

"Did she ask if I want to go with them?
I mean, it's a long way and —"

My aunt reaches over
and puts her hand on mine.
Holds it there.
Tears fill her eyes

as she shakes her head
ever so slightly.

My mother is not a mermaid.
My mother is not kind
or caring.
My mother doesn't
choose her children
above all else.

And yet
day after
day after
day,
I keep wishing
she'd change.

It's hard to
stop believing
in mermaids.

88 | Colby

IT'S TUESDAY. Tomorrow morning, Benny leaves for Atlanta.

After we've eaten dinner, I call his mom.

"I can't say good-bye," I tell her. "I'm sorry. I'd probably lose it."

She chuckles. "It's okay for boys to cry, you know."

"I guess. But we're tough, me and him."

"You've been through a lot together," she says.

"He's the best friend a guy could ask for. You tell him I said that, okay? And I'm gonna miss him like crazy."

"Now who's . . . Little . . . Miss . . . Sunshine?"

I shake my head. Of course she wouldn't let me off that easy. "Hey, Benny. Your mom gave you the phone, huh?"

"It's on speaker," she says.

"Oh. Right. Well, you guys have a safe trip, okay? And I'll see you soon. I know you're gonna bust balls and do what you gotta do to get back on your feet, man."

"Pynes?" he says.

"Yeah?"

"Take . . . state."

I close my eyes and put my head in my hands. "It's not easy, playing without you. But you know we're doing our best. We're gonna do everything we can to make it happen, that's for sure."

"Believe."

I laugh. "Oh, you gonna be like Coach now, huh? What was it you said? We're not a bunch of girls with confidence issues, are we?"

I hear a chuckle. "Take state," he says again.

"I hear ya, man. I hear ya. Look, I gotta go. Homework's calling and all that."

"We'll stay in touch, Colby," Mrs. Lewis says. "We'll try to call once a week or so."

"Sounds good. Hey, Benny?"

"Yeah?"

"Just so you know, there is one thing I believe in. More than anything else in the whole world right now." I swallow hard. "You."

"Bye, Colby."

"Bye, Benny."

I set down the phone. And then I let myself lose it.

89 : Lauren

TUESDAY

"You seem down, Lauren. I've heard the bake sale was a huge success, so it can't be that."

"No. It's not."

"What's on your mind?"

"I was thinking about the time I got lost in the grocery store."

Dr. Springer smiles. "Ah. I think everyone has one of those stories. Tell me yours."

When I started coming here, because Josh and Erica made me, back in August, I wouldn't have told her. But it's easier now, talking with her. I've told her more than I ever thought I would.

"It was a few days before Valentine's Day. I was around six or seven, so I knew it was a special day. A day of love. We went to the drugstore to buy boxes of valentines for my school party. As we were heading toward the register, I saw a huge display of candy. You know, boxes and boxes of hearts. And I wanted one so badly. I wanted someone to love me enough to buy me one of those boxes of candy. I asked my mom if she would buy me one, and she said no.

"She tried to pull me along, away from the display, but I was mad. I didn't want to go. I wanted a box of candy. I never threw fits about that kind of thing, ever, so I don't know why it made me so upset.

"Finally my mom said, fine, you stay there, I'll go get the other things I need, pay for everything, and come back for you.

"I stood there and tried to imagine what the chocolates looked like. What they tasted like. Were they all the same or was each one different? I kept trying to think of a way to get my mom to buy a box. I got so excited when I had the brilliant idea to ask my mom if she'd give me money so I could buy one for *her*. I'd tell her I wanted to get her one to show how much I loved her. That way, I could at least *see* the chocolates. And maybe, I thought, she'd be nice and let me have one.

"But she didn't come back. At least, not as quickly as I thought she would. So I went looking for her. And I couldn't find her." My throat tightens. Tears prick the back of my eyes. "Just as I was about to find a store employee and let them know I needed help because I was all alone, my mother showed up. I started crying when I saw her and tried to hug her, but she wouldn't have any of it."

"Did she say anything?" she asks.

"Not right away. She marched to the car with me running after her. I kept telling her how sorry I was. Over and over again. Once we were on our way toward home, she told me, 'Love isn't about chocolate. Love is about listening to your mother and being a good girl. And next time she tells you to do something, you better do it. Or you'll have to go find someone else who will love you.'"

I look out the window, blinking the tears back.

"Not a very loving thing to say, is it?" Dr. Springer says.

"No."

"What caused you to remember that? Do you know?"

I clear my throat as I look at Dr. Springer. "She called my aunt and uncle and told them she's moving. All the way across the country. I was thinking about how she's finally following through on that threat."

"Did she say why?"

"No. But she didn't ask me to come with her." I lean forward. "Do you think it's because of the social worker?"

"Actually, there's been an interesting development. Did you know Matthew's father was seeking custody?"

My hand flies to my mouth. "No. I had no idea."

"Do you know him?"

"Yeah. His name's Dwight. I like him. He's a pretty nice guy. Owns a landscaping business and lives next door to his parents, in an older neighborhood. He was around a lot until one day, early in the summer, he just . . . wasn't. She wouldn't tell me any details, only that they'd broken up."

"Well, Matthew is apparently living with Dwight now."

"Oh my God. Are you serious?"

"Yes. I don't have any details to share. I'm sure you have lots of questions, but that's all the information I have."

I try to take it all in. What it means. For Matthew. For my mom. For me.

"I'm going to call Dwight when I get home," I tell her. "Maybe Josh and Erica will drive me up to Washington to see Matthew."

"That's a good idea."

"But that means my mom is going to North Carolina alone," I say, thinking out loud.

Dr. Springer doesn't say anything. She probably knows I'm trying to process it all. Mostly, I just keep wondering the same things: Why does my mother want to go so far away? Why doesn't she want me to go with her? I don't understand. Does she really hate me that much?

I wish I could turn off all my feelings. Why can't I be more like her? I don't want to care, and yet I do. How is it so easy for her to simply not care?

The more I think of her just up and leaving me, forever, my chest tightens. I close my eyes as a couple of tiny tears slip out. Quietly. The same way my mom wants to slip away, right out of my life.

Part 4

. . . .

People live like birds in the woods:
When the time comes, each must take flight.
— CHINESE PROVERB

90 Colby

WE'RE GOING.

In two short weeks, we're going to the state championships. We won last night's semifinal game in overtime, with a field goal.

I gotta say, it was pretty damn sweet.

The game was a couple of hours away, but it seemed like the entire town caravanned there with us. The stadium was packed.

When we got home, it was late, and everyone was dog-tired. So we agreed to meet up tonight to celebrate. We're going back to Murphy's Hill. It'll be the first time we've all been there since Benny got hurt.

After I wake up, I go to the kitchen to get a bottle of water, and find Dad at the kitchen table with his laptop. Scattered all over the table are college brochures.

"Where's Gram and Grandpa?"

"Grocery shopping."

"How come you're not at work?"

"I put the assistant manager of the store in charge so I could have the day off. Thought we could spend some time together, talking about teams and schools. You know, get this thing figured out. I think it's time for you to make your decision."

I groan. "Dad, I have to get ready for work. I can't do this today. Anyway, can't we wait until football season is over? I'll have a lot more time then."

"Damn. I didn't think about the fact that you might be working today. Could you call and let Mr. Weir know you can't make it in this afternoon? I bet he'll understand. Everyone's so happy about going to state, you can do no wrong."

I shake my head. "Dad —"

"This is important, Colby."

"I know, but . . ." I sigh as I rub my face. "I can't bail on Mr. Weir. He's counting on me. And you can't just swoop in anytime you want and tell me to drop everything. It's not fair."

I head toward the bathroom.

"Tomorrow, then," he calls out. "We're doing this tomorrow, like it or not."

"Fine," I mutter under my breath. Even though it's not fine.

I just don't know how to tell him that.

91 Lauren

MY BABY brother
is not such a baby
any longer.

When I crouched down,
arms open wide,
heart open wider,
Matthew toddled across the
room until he was close
enough for me
to scoop him up
and squeeze him tight.

Cheek to cheek,
we twirled around,
our giggles the
perfect music for
the spontaneous dance.

I stroked his hair,
his face, and
every little pudgy roll
on his arms and legs.

Oh, how my mother
must miss him, I thought.

Matthew and I played
with balls and blocks,
and I read him books
as I bounced him
on my knees.

Aunt Erica and I
got up before the birds
last Saturday and drove
the five hours so I could see him.

Dwight said I could
come and see him
anytime I'd like.

If only it weren't
such a long way from
Willow to Seattle.

Before we left,
to head back home,
I asked Erica if I
could try calling my mom.

Maybe she would see me.
Maybe I could talk her into staying.
Maybe with my help, our family could be together again.

I dialed the number.

It rang
and rang
and rang.

Her voice
startled me,
I hadn't heard it
in so long.

"I can't take your call.
Leave a message."

Beep.

"Hi, Mom.
It's me. Lauren.
I was hoping to talk to you.
Have you moved yet?
Can you maybe call me?
Thanks.
Bye."

After all the kisses
I could give my brother,
we drove home.

I pretended to sleep,
guilt covering me
like a blanket.

I screwed it all up for us
the night I called the cops.

Now here it is,
a week later,
and everyone in Willow
has football fever
except me.

They are happy
to be winning
while I'm sad
about everything
I've lost.

92 : Colby

THE PARTY at Murphy's Hill is going strong when I get there. There are so many cars parked along the old lumber road, it feels like half the school must have come out to celebrate.

It's a clear night. Cool. The almost-full moon glows in the sky, giving out a fair amount of light.

Derek points me to the keg when I walk up to him and a bunch of other guys. "But if you drink, you have to hand over your keys," he tells me. "We've got designated drivers tonight."

"Great," I tell him. "But I don't feel like drinking."

He nods, like he understands. But he doesn't. Not really. Everyone's laughing and having a good time, and I want to feel happy, like I did right after the game, but I don't.

All I feel is pressure.

Pressure to win the game. Pressure to choose the right college. Pressure to play and make my dad happy. Pressure to do right by Benny. Pressure to be the person everyone expects me to be.

It's like I'm at one end of an old, rickety bridge between two cliffs, way up high. The bridge sways back and forth in the wind, and as I look out, it seems pretty much impossible to make it across to the other side.

If I go, what happens?

If I stand my ground, what happens?

Everything's so mixed up right now.

"Hey," I hear from behind me as someone taps me on the shoulder.

I turn around, away from the small group of guys I'm standing with. "Hi," I say to Lauren and Stasia.

"Great game last night," Stasia says. "You were amazing."

"Thanks." I feel like I should say more, but I don't.

Stasia looks past me and waves at someone. "There's Sam," she says, smiling. "Think I'll go say hi."

"You know," I say to Lauren before Stasia leaves, "I think I might go for a drive. You girls want to come?"

Lauren looks at Stasia. "You two go," Stasia says. "If you need a ride home, Lauren, just be back here by twelve."

"Okay. Thanks."

Stasia squeezes Lauren's hand before she takes off. "Be safe."

Lauren and I head down the hill.

"I didn't drink anything," I tell her. "You know, in case you were wondering."

"I figured," she said. "I mean, I didn't think you were the type to risk my life like that." I can feel her looking at me. Studying me. Then quietly she says, "Don't worry. I trust you."

It feels good to hear her say that. To know that someone believes I'm doing the right thing.

We get to my truck, and I go to her side and unlock the door with the help of the flashlight app on my phone. She hops in, and as I start to close the door, she puts her arm out. "Hey. Are you okay?"

"Honestly? Right this minute, I'm actually doing pretty good."

"Me too," she says with a little smile.

93 | Lauren

THE STARS twinkle as we drive.
We listen to music. Mumford & Sons.

We don't say anything.
It's not awkward. It's nice.

He drives farther and farther
out into the country.

Past farmhouses that have
stood a hundred years.

Past fields of horses and cows,
goats and sheep.

Past barns where owls hunt
and tiny mice scurry about.

When he finally comes to
a stop sign, he makes a U-turn.

"Do you know where
you're going?" I ask.

He sounds almost sad
when he says, "Not a clue."

94 | Colby

"DRIVING AIMLESSLY is a good talent to have when you live in a small town," I explain. "Sometimes there's just nothing else to do but drive."

"But there's a party going on," she says.

"True. Except everyone's so annoyingly happy there."

She laughs. "Colby, you're going to state! That's a good reason to be happy, isn't it? Or did I miss the part where you broke your leg and can't play?"

It makes me think of Benny, hurt and unable to play. And as soon as she's said it, I know she thinks of him too. "Sorry," she says. "I was trying to be funny. I didn't mean —"

"Don't worry about it. You're absolutely right. I should be happy."

"So how come you're not?"

I turn down another back road and go in a different direction, toward the tree farm Dad and I visit every year to cut down our Christmas tree.

"I don't know," I finally reply. "It's not that I'm *unhappy* we're going to state. There's just . . . a lot going on right now."

"Can I ask you something?"

"Sure."

"What do you want out of life right now? I mean, what do you *really* want?"

"Bugles sound good, actually. Got any on you?"

She lightly slaps my arm. "Come on. Be serious. I want to know."

I slow down and turn into Wicker's Christmas Tree Farm. It's set back from the road a ways with a gravel parking lot and then behind it, acres and acres of Noble and Douglas firs. I park in a spot that isn't too visible from the main road. I turn the engine off but keep the radio and headlights on.

"It's a complicated question. Too hard to think about and drive at the same time," I explain as I turn the volume down on the stereo.

"Do you get your tree here?" she asks, looking out the front window at shadows of trees that go on for miles.

"We do. My dad says my mom always insisted on a fresh-cut tree. I don't think my dad really cares where the tree comes from. But I get the feeling we come out here as a way to honor her memory at Christmastime."

"That's sweet. He must have really loved her."

"Yeah. I think so."

"Maybe that's what you want. Maybe you want your mom here right now, to help you sort stuff out."

"Maybe." I pause. "Is that what you want?"

"Maybe."

"Is this one of those games where maybe means yes, and no means yes, but yes means no?" I ask.

"No."

I smile. "Is that a yes, then?"

My lame attempt to change the subject doesn't work. "Here's what I think," she says, settling back into the seat, curling one of her legs up onto the seat with her. "I think we both want the same thing. Deep down, the same exact thing."

"What?"

"For our families to accept us, just as we are."

"Is that why you moved here?" I ask.

She chews on a thumbnail. "If you want to know the truth, my mom got really pissed at me."

"So, coming here was your punishment?"

"Kind of." She pauses. "She basically kicked me out. Helped me find somewhere else to go, and then she made me leave."

"Jesus, Lauren. I'm sorry."

"Now she's moving across the country, and I'm not sure what's going to happen to me."

"You'll stay where you are, right?"

"I don't know. I'm pretty sure when Josh and Erica said I could stay with them, they didn't intend for me to become, like, their fourth child."

We're both quiet for a minute. Then she says, "But we weren't talking about me. We were talking about you. You never really answered my question. What do you want?"

I scratch my head. "I don't know how to answer that."

"All right, let's break it down. Do you want to win state?"

"Yes. For Benny. And for my team, I want to win state. But . . ."

"But what?"

"If we win state, I think that means I have to play college ball. The pressure will be on like nobody's business. Everyone will expect me to play."

"And you're sure you don't want to play?"

"Positive."

"But you want to go to college?" she asks.

"Yeah. I want to study civil engineering." I look at her.

"And you're going to go to become a whatever it is that studies birds, right?"

"I don't know now. With my living situation up in the air, how does that work? For financial aid, I mean. I bet my mom is still claiming me as a dependent, which means I need her to help me fill out the financial aid forms. And that's never gonna happen."

"Maybe your aunt and uncle can write a letter and explain the situation."

She sighs. "Like they don't have enough going on with their jobs and family and everything else."

"I think you should talk to them," I tell her. "I don't know your aunt very well, but your uncle is a super-nice guy. Let them help you figure it out."

"So, do you go to the bookstore a lot?"

I shrug. "Maybe. Okay, yes, I do. So?"

She smiles. "A football player who reads. Man, that is . . ."

"What?"

"Never mind."

"Tell me."

"I can't."

"Yes, you can." I reach over and start tickling her side. "Tell me. It's what?"

She laughs and tries to push me away, but I hold her with one hand and continue to tickle with the other. "Okay, okay, it's hot!" she gasps.

I stop and lean back. "Is that really what you were going to say?"

She straightens her shirt. "Maybe."

I reach for her again and she squeals, pushing herself

back toward the door. "Yes, yes, okay? Geez, don't let it go to your head."

Before I have a chance to change my mind, I tell her, "Well, you're not bad yourself."

"Thanks," she says softly.

I'm about to start up the truck and get the hell out of here because it has gone from zero to a hundred on the uncomfortable scale, when she scoots over next to me.

She's right there. Looking at me. And it's pretty obvious what's coming next. The thing is, I want that too. I've wanted it for weeks. But at the same time, I don't want to ruin what we have. Besides, my focus on the field has been good. Really good. I'm doing what I need to do.

"I don't want to mess anything up," I tell her before I realize that probably doesn't make any sense to her.

"I know," she says, like she completely understands. "And I promise you won't."

And then she touches my cheek, leans in, and kisses me.

95 : Lauren

WHEN I say
"I promise,"
it is really
a promise
to myself
more than it is
to him.

Nothing else
can happen
until after
the championship.

Tonight,
while we were
driving,
I could see
how much
pressure
he's under.

I don't want
to add to that.

I won't
add to that.

Not right now.

But I wanted him
to know how I feel.

I wanted him
to know,
in no uncertain terms,
how much I care about him.

That no matter what
happens at the end
of these two weeks,
whether he wins or loses,
it won't change
how I feel about him.

Words have
this way of getting
mixed up
when we're trying
too hard.

I didn't want
to take that chance.

They say a picture
is worth a
thousand words.

I bet a kiss
is worth
ten times that.

You can say
so much
with so little.

96 | Colby

HOLY SHIT.

It finally happened.

And what do you know, I let myself kiss her and managed to ignore the alarms going off in my head: Danger! Danger! Step away from the girl! Step AWAY from the girl!

It was *really* nice.

When we're done, she scoots over to the other side of the seat and buckles up. "We should probably go," she says. "It's getting late."

"Oh. Right." I turn the engine on and start backing out of the gravel road.

"Is everything okay?" she asks, for the second time tonight.

This time, I answer more enthusiastically. "Yes. Everything's great!"

She chuckles. "Okay, Sunny Bunny."

I look over at her. "Did you just call me Sunny Bunny? Man, Benny calls me Little Miss Sunshine. What is it with you people?"

"Well, my mom used to call me Sunny Bunny. I think you're a lot like me. Always trying to keep things positive, for the sake of other people."

I think you're a lot like me.

I recall the words she said earlier. *I think we both want the same thing.*

Are we really that much alike? Is that why it's so easy being with her?

We drive toward town, silence filling up the space between us. I turn the music back up.

"You're taking me home?" she asks as we drive past Murphy's Hill.

"Yeah. Is that okay? Or did you want to go back to the party?"

"No. Home's fine." Pause. "It feels weird calling it that. I mean, because it's not my home. Not really."

"Sure it is."

"Why do you say that?"

"You live there with people who care about you." I shrug. "That's home."

She doesn't say anything.

"It'll be all right, Lauren. You'll see."

97 Lauren

WHEN HE pulls into
the Jiffy Mart
parking lot,
I can't help but laugh.

"My treat," he says.
"Get whatever you want."

I know
a convenience store
is about as far
from romantic
as you can get,
but I am truly touched
by how hard he's trying
to make me happy.

"What sounds good to you?"
I ask as he opens the door for me
and helps me out of his truck.

"Bugles and a slushie.
You?"

"Same."

"Copycat."

We stand there,
in the middle of
the parking lot,
just inches away
from each other.

"But I liked Bugles first," I say,
"so I think you're the copycat."

"Crap. You're right."
We walk toward
the door and he says,
"So, the friends thing.
It's over now, right?
Man, I knew it'd be too hard."

He starts to put his arm
around my shoulders,
but I duck and turn.

"It's not over," I tell him.

He stops. "It's not?"

"No.
Not until you win state."

He crosses his arms.
"Have you been talking to my dad?"

"Colby, you have a lot on your mind.
Get through the next couple of weeks.
Then we can . . . pick up where we left off."

"But —"

"I promised I wouldn't let
you mess anything up.
This is how I do that."

We go around the store,
getting our snacks.

"Two weeks?" he asks
when we get to the register.

"Two weeks.
Saturday night.
Your favorite restaurant."

"What if we don't win?" he asks.

I smile.
"I'm in no matter what."

98 | Colby

"TWO WEEKS is a long time," I say on the way to her aunt and uncle's house.

She takes a drink of her blue-raspberry slushie. "It really isn't."

"I think it is."

"It'll fly by. You'll see."

"I was a good friend, wasn't I?" I ask.

She laughs. "The best. Until tonight, when you couldn't keep your hands off me."

"Hey, you're the one —"

She throws a couple of Bugles at me. "Stop. We shouldn't be talking about this."

"So why'd you do it? Get my hopes up like that?" I pull into the driveway and put the truck into park.

"Colby, I didn't get your hopes up."

"You didn't?"

"No. Look at it this way. Instead of dreading the game that could change your life in a hundred different ways, now you can't wait for it. Right?"

Oh my God. She's right.

"You're brilliant." She nods as she opens the door and hops out. "Hey, Lauren?"

"Yeah?"

"I'm really glad I ran into you tonight. It's just what I needed."

"Me too. Good night."

"Good night."

As I head home, I realize for once in a long, long time, I feel like everything is going to be all right.

Sunny Bunny. That's me.

99 : Lauren

SUNDAY,
the kids
wake me up
early because
we're going
to the zoo.

I've never been
to a zoo.
Not one time.
But I don't
tell them that.

It's funny how
they don't even
ask me if I want
to go, they just
assume I do.

And they're right.

We play
the license plate

game on the drive
to Portland.

Andrew's really
good at it,
often the first
to find the letter
we're looking for.

Once inside
the zoo gates,
I see every animal
through little
Demi's eyes.

The chimps are cute.
The bears are scary.
The penguins are funny.
The elephants are big!

The baby elephant, Lily,
doesn't stray far from
her mother, Rose.

When Rose reaches
her trunk over and
rests it on Lily's
back for a moment,
a sweet sign of affection,
the crowd lets out
a collective "aw."

I feel my heart
breaking
a little more.

What I wouldn't give
for a little bit
of motherly love
like that.

100 : Colby

SUNDAY MORNING, as I'm lying there checking my phone, it rings.

"Hello?"

"Hey."

"Benny! How are you?"

"Pretty good."

"You sound great! I've been thinking about you. Wasn't sure of the best time to call. You heard about the game?"

"Yeah. Awesome."

"Well, it was all for you."

He doesn't say anything.

"I miss you, man," I tell him. "Are things going well?"

"Working hard."

"Good! I know you are. I can't wait until you come home and things are back to the way they were before."

"Won't ever . . . be the same," he says.

The way he says it, it feels like someone is ripping my chest wide open. "No, I guess not. But you gotta know, everyone wants you to come home, Benny. When you're ready, of course."

Again, he doesn't say anything, so I keep talking.

"I have to decide what to do about college. Soon. The recruiters are starting to breathe down my neck again, with the season winding down, and my dad is about ready to kill me if I don't make up my mind. I don't know what to do."

After it's out, I regret it. I shouldn't be griping about this with him. What he wouldn't give to have recruiters breathing down his neck.

"Sorry, Ben —"

"You know . . . what to do."

It makes me laugh. "I do?"

"Deep down. You know."

I swallow hard.

"Listen," he says. "Just . . . listen."

"But I'm scared," I say, in almost a whisper.

"It's your life," he says. "Live it. Be happy."

"What about you? Are you ever gonna be happy again?"

"Yes. I'm happy. Now."

"Now?"

"I'm alive. So lucky. I'm happy. Want that . . . for you."

I can't believe this conversation. It should be me telling *him* to be happy. Look at all he's lost. Instead, I'm the miserable one, and for what?

"Going to state hasn't really changed anything for me," I tell him. "I don't want to play college ball."

"More to life . . . than football."

"Benny, is this really you, or is this someone pretending to be you?"

"It's me."

"You're different," I tell him.

"Yeah. I'm looking . . . at community colleges now. Want to do something . . . in the medical field. You know. Help people. Gives me . . . something to . . . work for."

"Oh man. Benny. That's great. You can do it. I know you can."

"Working hard," he says again.

"So. You gonna tell me to win state?"

"Nope."

"How come?"

"You got . . . enough pressure. Won't do that . . . to you."

"Yeah."

"Be happy, Pynes." He pauses. "Promise?"

I close my eyes. "I promise."

101 ┊ Lauren

AS WE head
back toward
Willow and
away from the zoo
and the big city of Portland,
the topic of
conversation
is where to stop
for dinner.

Everyone's
hungry.

No one can
agree.

No one
knows
what
happens
next.

It's a tense
few minutes.

Just like Colby.
Just like me.
Neither one of us
knows what
happens next.

It's hard to be
happy in the now
when you can't
stop worrying
about the future.

What I want
is to trust that
everything will
work out.
To believe
with all my heart
that I'll end up
where I belong.

We end up
stopping at
a twenty-four-hour diner.

No one complains.
Everyone's just happy

to be somewhere
with food.

Everything
worked out.

We ended up
somewhere,
together,
and that's
what really
matters.

102 : Colby

HE MAKES it sound so easy.

Be happy.

Like you can just get everyone on your side and happiness will magically appear, no problem. Still, I promised. I've got to figure out my next move. There's no one to coach me on this one. I'm on my own.

I'm about to head toward the bathroom to take a shower, when Dad rushes into my room.

"Colby, get dressed. An ambulance is on its way. Something's wrong with your gram."

I stand there in total panic. "What do you mean something's wrong?"

"She might be having a heart attack. I don't know. Just . . . get dressed. I'm going outside to wait for the ambulance."

He leaves and I throw on the clothes I wore last night.

I stand in the hallway, hesitant. What should I do? I want to see her and yet there's a part of me that's afraid. I don't know if I can stand to see her in pain.

I take a deep breath and walk to their room. The door is slightly ajar. I can hear Grandpa talking.

"You're doing great, Judith. Nice, slow breaths. Help will be here in a minute."

I open the door and step in. She's in her robe, lying on the floor. "Gram?" I kneel down next to her. Her eyes are closed, and it's like each breath takes everything she's got.

She opens her eyes and looks like she's going to say something, but I put my finger on her lips. They feel cold. "Shhh, don't talk. Save your energy. I just want you to know, I love you, Gram. Everything's going to be all right. Hang on, okay?"

She closes her eyes again.

I watch her chest. Up. Down. Up. Down.

I will it to keep moving.

We hear the sirens a minute or so later. Dad comes in and yells, "They're here!"

Grandpa's eyes meet mine. He looks so worried, so scared, it makes me want to cry.

"We need to get out of the way, Colby," Grandpa says. "They'll need room to get the stretcher in here."

We both stand up, but we don't move. She looks so helpless. So . . . alone.

Grandpa reaches out and takes my hand. Together, we step toward the other side of the room, just as the paramedics come in. He squeezes my hand before he lets it go.

"Who can tell us what happened?" one of the guys asks.

Grandpa steps forward and starts talking. She'd taken a bath. A long one. When she got out, she called for him. Told Grandpa she didn't feel well. Nauseous. And said she felt like someone was sitting on her chest.

As one of the paramedics begins to undress her to take her vitals, I realize I shouldn't be watching.

I turn around, my arms squeezed tightly to my chest. I look out their bedroom window. It's gray and dreary outside. Raining.

Gram loves the rain.

I blink the tears back.

103 Lauren

THAT NIGHT, Demi asks
me to tuck her in.

Her mom's taking a nap
because she has to work later.

Uncle Josh finishes the story,
kisses her good night, then leaves us.

"How do you like to be
tucked in?" I ask her.

"Do it the way your
mommy did it to you," she says.

"My mommy never
tucked me in," I explain.

"Okay. Get in and
I will show you how," she says.

She hops up, throws the covers
back, and pulls me into her bed.

"You take the covers like this,"
she says, bringing them to my chin.

"Then you tuck one side and
say, 'Good night, sleep tight,'

and tuck the other side and
say, 'Don't let the bedbugs bite.'

And then you give a kiss
on the forehead, like this. *Mwah.*

Before you leave, you say,
'I love you with all my heart.'"

"That's so cool," I say.
"You are a very lucky girl."

Demi crawls into her bed
and I tuck her in, like she showed me.

After I say, "I love you with all my heart,"
she says, "I'm happy you're part of our family."

She rolls over to get comfy. I turn off the lamp.
And as I head toward the door, I whisper, "Me too."

104 Colby

"IT'S NOT supposed to be her in there," Grandpa says as we sit in the waiting room. "She's not like me. She's the strong one. The healthy one."

"Dad, don't do that," my dad says. "These things happen."

"She was always worrying about me," Grandpa says. "I should have been paying more attention. Made sure she was taking care of herself too. Did she even have a physical this past year? I can't remember. Damn it. I don't remember."

He rubs his face with his hands, and I wish I could say something to make him feel better. The thing is, I feel bad too. How many times did I ask how Grandpa was feeling, never thinking to ask Gram? We all just assumed she was fine. Took her and everything she did for us for granted.

I stand up and stretch. I'm tired of sitting. Tired of this waiting room, where I've spent far too much time the last few months. Tired of being reminded how things can change on a dime.

"I'm gonna go outside," I tell them. "Get some fresh air."

Grandpa jumps up. "I'll go with you." He looks at Dad. "If you hear anything, come and find us?"

Dad nods. "Of course."

We make our way to the courtyard, passing all kinds of different people. One thing's for sure. None of them look very happy to be here.

Grandpa opens the door when we reach the outdoor space. We step out, and the first thing I notice is that everything's wet, since it's been raining on and off all day. That includes the benches and chairs. It's a nice space, flower beds landscaped among the concrete.

"Do you want to sit down?" Grandpa asked. "I can go get some paper towels and wipe a bench down for us."

"I'm tired of sitting," I say. "But if you want to . . ."

"No. I'm fine. You're right. It's good to stand for a while."

We make our way to the very middle of the courtyard, and I look up. Nothing to see but gray sky.

"You've seen too much of this place lately, Colby," Grandpa says.

I stuff my hands in my pockets. "That's for sure."

"How's Benny doing?"

"I talked to him this morning. He sounds good."

"That's great. I bet he'll be back home in no time."

"I hope so."

"You know, I'm proud of you, Colby," he says. "These last few months haven't been easy, and look at you. Going to state. Choosing a college soon. You didn't just keep it together, you've excelled."

"Grandpa, right now, I couldn't care less about that championship game."

"I understand. But there are a lot of people in this town who do care. A lot. And you know your gram and I will be there, cheering you on. Nothing will keep her away."

"We don't know that," I say.

We're quiet for a minute. Then he says, "You know, when bad things happen, it's good to have something else to think about. Something to believe in. Whether it's a terrible motor-cycle accident, or a heart attack, your team and the dedication you all show to one another and this town reminds people that there is more good in the world than bad."

I shake my head. "I know how much our town loves us. But sometimes, when I'm thinking about it, and all the other stuff going on in the world, I want to scream at people, it's just a game. Find something better to believe in. Something that *really* matters, you know?"

"Oh, Colby. You know it matters. It matters because it brings the town together in a way nothing else does. Friends and family, all together, sending their love to one another, and to you. All of you, on that field, representing us. It's not just a game. It's a community, and everything that represents. And you may leave here someday and never look back, I don't know, but I can tell you one thing. You will always remember this town and what it was like to be a part of it. Maybe now it feels small and stifling, but I bet someday, you'll see it differently. Tight-knit. Cozy. And most of all, home."

I look at my grandpa, trying so hard to convince me that what I do on that field matters. Because it's not just everyone else in this town that needs something to believe in; I need it too.

But what if I can't anymore?

I reach back and pull out my wallet. I read the card I've read when I've went to buy gas for my truck or a slushie at the Jiffy Mart or something for Gram at the grocery store, so I'd save her a trip.

I believe.

I believe in myself.

I believe in the team.

I believe it's our time.

Maybe it's these words that got us to state.

But when state's over, what happens then? What the hell am I supposed to believe in then?

WE ARE all tiptoeing
around it.

"We" being me,
Uncle Josh,
and Aunt Erica.

"It" being
the conversation
we need to have,
about what happens now.

With me.

My therapist says
I just need to ask them
if I can stay and if
they'll help me with
college applications
for next year.

Just ask.

Like it's as easy
as asking for a drink
of water when I'm thirsty.

For days and weeks,
I try to get up the
courage to say,
"Can we talk?"

And just when
it seems it might be
the right time,
Thursday night,
the day before
the big game,
the phone rings.

It's Mom.

106 : Colby

A MILD heart attack. After tests and more tests, that's what they called it. With medications, a good diet, and regular walking, the doctor says Gram will be fine.

She stayed at the hospital a couple of days for monitoring, and then they sent her home.

Dad took the week off from work so Grandpa wouldn't overdo it, taking care of her. The doctor said Gram would be tired the first week, but she should still get up, get dressed, and should not lie in bed all day.

I'm pretty sure when he said that, he didn't know that lying in bed all day is about the last thing my gram would ever want to do.

With everything going on, Dad doesn't mention the big "college decision," and I certainly don't bring it up. I'm thankful for the reprieve. My plan is to get through the final game, and worry about the rest later. Cross that bridge when I come to it, so to speak.

By the second week, Gram seems back to her old self, though we only let her cook dinner for us, while we take care of our own breakfasts and lunches. We're also doing our own laundry, which bugs the crap out of her, because none of us does it the "right" way.

I honestly don't care if I pull my wrinkly jeans out of the

dryer after they've sat there for two days, but Gram cares. And she lets me know it.

I just smiled when she told me how I should have been doing it, and when she finished giving me my laundry lesson, I said, "I'm so glad you're feeling better, Gram."

She replied, "Well, honestly, I'll be glad when I can do your laundry again, so it's done right. You deserve better than wrinkled pants, Colby!"

I gave her a big hug as I laughed about it.

Now it's Thursday, and we're dressing for our last practice of the season. Tomorrow night, we'll be up in Portland, in a big fancy locker room, getting ready for the game of our lives.

I jump when I hear Coach holler, "Gather round!"

"What's this?" Derek asks. "The big motivating speech comes tomorrow night, doesn't it?"

Coach smiles. "Yes. It does. But this afternoon I have some good news to share. I just got off the phone and wanted to tell you we'll have some special guests at the game tomorrow night."

We look at one another, question marks floating over our heads.

"There's no way you'll guess, so I'll just tell you. Your teammate, Benny Lewis, is flying in tomorrow for the game."

The room erupts in cheers. I'm sitting there in shock, wondering why Benny didn't let me know about this.

"Lewis has made incredible progress," Coach goes on. "His mom told me the overseeing physician says it's nothing short of a miracle. Anyway, I've been checking in with his family on a regular basis, and it was my hope that I could help to make this happen for you boys. His team of medical staff agreed to let him fly home, just for the weekend. On Sunday, he'll return to Atlanta, because his work there certainly isn't finished."

Coach looks around at us for a minute before he says, "I know this has been a challenging season for y'all. I wouldn't have blamed you if you fell apart, if you couldn't muster the strength and courage week after week like a winning team needs to. But you did it. And I am so damn proud of each and every one of you. And I know whatever happens tomorrow night, you're gonna make Benny proud too.

"Now let's get out there and have a good practice. I'll see you on the field in five."

107 Lauren

SHE WANTS us
back together.

"I want us to be a family again."

That's what she told me.

Now I'm trying to tell
Erica and Josh this.

When I told them I'd
just talked to my mom,
they ushered the kids
to the playroom,
like a flock of ducklings,
then took me into the
family room.

"What did she say?"
Erica asks as I sit
back on the sofa,
trying to digest
the brief conversation.

I stare at the coffee
table, the rings left there
by glasses of juice
because kids
aren't careful about
things like coasters.

"Lauren?" Josh says.

I look at him.

"She wants me to come to North Carolina.
Just for a while. Then we're going to
go back to Seattle. She wants to fight
for shared custody of Matthew."

Josh and Erica look at
each other. I can tell they're
not sure what to say.

"She says she needs me.
That she can't do it without me.
I don't know the details,
why she didn't get shared custody
in the first place, but she said
she regrets that she didn't fight harder.
She said she misses him."

I stare at the rings again
and think of Andrew, Henry,

and Demi. Those are their
rings. On their table.
In their family room, where
they watch SpongeBob
and laugh, like a family does.

"And that was it?" Josh asks.

"She told me she was sorry," I reply.
"For everything."

Erica talks slowly.
"Lauren, it's a big decision.
Nothing has to be decided right now.
Think on it for a while, okay?"

"But they're my family," I say.
"I belong with them."

"Let me call her," Josh says.
"I want to talk to her about this."

I stand up. "Fine. But I'm going to pack.
I have money saved.
I'm going to buy a ticket."

Josh stands. "Of course we'll
help with whatever you need.
But let's wait a few days.
You know, think on it awhile."

I shake my head.
They don't understand.
I can't wait.

She might change her mind.

108 Colby

BENNY MUST have wanted to surprise me. He didn't tell me because he wanted me to be surprised along with everyone else.

Just like he wanted to surprise his mom on her birthday. He's still the same good-hearted guy. And I can't wait to see him. See how he's doing. What he looks like. I keep wondering if he'll come in a wheelchair, or if he's able to walk by himself now. I didn't want to ask him any of these questions on the phone. I mean, the last thing I'd want to do is make the guy feel like a failure if he isn't able to walk yet. I have no idea what's normal and what's not, and from what his mom said, it sounds like there are lots of degrees of normal, anyway.

I'm kind of a wreck on Friday. Between the game looming large and the thought of getting to see my best friend for the first time in weeks, I can hardly sit still in my morning classes.

And then, as I'm heading to the cafeteria for lunch, I get a text. From a number I don't recognize.

> My mom called. I'm leaving tonight. Can I see you
> before I go? Lauren

I blink a few times, reread the message over and over. At first I wonder if it's some sort of cruel joke. I decide there's only one way to find out.

I move into a corner of the hallway and call the number.

"Hello?"

"Lauren?"

"Hi, Colby."

"It is you. I wasn't sure."

"I borrowed my aunt's phone."

"So it's true? You're leaving?"

"Yeah. Taking the red-eye tonight."

It feels like someone's punched me in the gut.

"I'll be right there."

109 Lauren

IN THE winter,
the sun shines less,
the temperatures
drop, and the
geese know
it is time.

It's not something
they consider,
as if they have a choice.

They don't ask questions.
They don't look around and wonder.
They don't consult others.

It's time,
and so they go.

They go
because it's
what they're
supposed to do.

And so it is
with me.

She's my mom.
He's my brother.
I belong with them.

I'm going
because it's
what I'm
supposed to do.

Sometimes we make choices.
Sometimes choices are made for us.
Either way, that's life, and
we just hope for the best.

110 Colby

I STOP at Walgreens on the way and make a mad dash around the place, getting everything I can. Then I practically fly to the McManns', hoping the whole way I can get her to change her mind.

When I get there, I ring the bell, holding the gift bag, and wait.

Mrs. McMann opens the door and I say hello.

Her eyes look sad. "Hi, Colby. Lauren's upstairs, packing. Come in."

I step in, and she shuts the door behind me.

"So, she's really leaving?" I ask.

She simply replies, "Yes."

"Does she have to go?" I ask. "I mean, could she stay here?"

"Well, I don't think she wants to stay here."

"No, she does. But she thinks you guys don't want her. I mean, not permanently, anyway."

She's about to respond when Lauren appears at the top of the stairs. "Hey, Colby. Come on up."

I give Mrs. McMann a quick glance before I head up the stairs.

I start to reach out, to give Lauren a hug, but she's already walking down the hallway. "You got here really fast. My room is down here, at the end."

I follow her. It's a big house. There are at least four bedrooms that we walk past.

When we get to her room, she plops down on her bed. Her suitcase is on the floor, full of clothes, but not zipped up yet.

"So what'd your mom say?" I ask.

"She said that she wants to be a family again. She wants to save up our money so we can move back to Seattle, and we're going to fight to get shared custody of my little brother."

"You want to go, then?"

"Of course."

"Did she apologize? Say she missed you? Anything?"

"Yeah. She apologized. In a general sort of way. I mean, I could tell she feels bad."

"Did she ask you how you've been?"

"You don't understand, Colby." She stands up and goes to her dresser, where she picks up a hair band and throws it in her suitcase. "She's not really like that. And don't make her out to be the bad guy in all of this. It's not entirely her fault. I made mistakes too. It's just a messed-up situation, and the important thing is that she wants to try and make it right."

I get up and go over to her. "But, Lauren —"

She doesn't let me finish. "Can I see what you brought me? We don't have all day, you know." She smiles, trying to lighten the mood. "Don't you have to catch a bus soon?"

I look at the clock on her nightstand and realize she's right. I texted Coach and told him I forgot something and had to run home, so I'd have to miss the spirit rally after lunch. Pretty sure he'll forgive me for that. Missing the team bus, however, would not make him happy.

I hand her the gift bag. She takes it and sits down on her bed again. One by one, she pulls the items out.

A bottle of blue nail polish.

A small picture of a vase of daisies.

Stickers of the sun and hot air balloons.

A paint-by-number set of three parrots.

A cupcake wrapped in cellophane.

And finally, a bag of Bugles.

"Oh, Colby," she whispers, tears in her eyes. "My favorite things."

"All except the bake sale."

She holds up the cupcake. "But something you'd find at a bake sale, yes?"

I nod. "Right."

She stands up and hugs me. "Thank you so much."

"Can you come to the game tonight?" I ask when we pull away. "Before your flight?"

She straightens the strings of my hoodie, avoiding my eyes. "I told them they could drop me off at the airport and then go to the game. That way, they don't have to risk missing any of it. I'll be there really early, but that's okay." She points at the bookcase full of books. "I have plenty of books to choose from."

"Lauren, you don't have to go, you know."

She takes my hand. "Yes, I do. I know you probably don't understand, but . . ."

"Is it really what you want?" I ask. "Just tell me that."

111 Lauren

WHAT I want
is for you
to build a bridge.

A bridge that
connects these
two parts of my
life so I don't
have to choose
one or the other.

I don't want to choose.

Because the thing about choices?

You get something
while you lose something else.

And if you choose wrong,
you risk losing

everything.

112 | Colby

SHE KISSES me. Softly. Slowly. It tastes like sadness. I wonder if all good-bye kisses taste that way.

Then she answers my question in an odd way. "Going to live with my family is what I have to do. What I want doesn't matter."

"Lauren, don't you see? What you want matters most of all. You don't *have* to."

She changes the subject. "I'm sorry to break our date tomorrow night."

I sigh. "Well, I did it to you first. I guess we're even now."

She's still holding my hand as she leads me to the door. "Thank you for the gifts. I'll paint the birds and send them to you. You can hang it in your locker." She tries to lighten the mood. "All the guys will be so jealous."

I reach out and hug her again. "I don't want to go," I whisper into her hair.

She pulls away. "You have a game to play, Number Twenty. The whole town is counting on you."

"Benny's flying in," I tell her. "For the game."

"Oh my gosh, that's awesome!" she says. "See, you won't miss me tomorrow night. You two will be up at Murphy's Hill. Just like old times."

I stare at her. "Lauren. I'm going to miss you. More than you know."

She bites her lip. Looks at the floor for a moment before she finally says, "You should really go."

"Stay in touch?" I ask.

She nods. "Absolutely."

"You promise?"

She holds up her hand, like she's swearing. "I promise."

It makes me think of my promise to Benny. To be happy. Right now, that seems completely and totally impossible.

113 ⋮ Lauren

WHEN JOSH and Erica
come to my room later,
they appear uneasy.

They sit and tell me
that we're making a big
mistake, rushing into this.

Josh called my mom
and talked to her some more.

"She's living with some guy she met online," he says.
"That's why she moved there.
Lauren, I think she's pretty messed up."

I argue with them. I tell them it's
because she's missing her family.
I try to convince myself
as much as I try to convince them.

They ask question after question,
like I'm on trial for murder.

No, I don't know for sure if she'll get Matthew back.
No, I don't know why he was taken away in the first place.
No, I don't know when we'll move back to Seattle.

Is it a crime to want to feel wanted?
Is it a crime to miss your little brother?
Is it a crime to try to fix your mistakes?

Finally I scream, "Why are you doing this?
They're my *family*. I belong with them!"

"But maybe you belong with us," Erica says softly,
like she has to be careful or
the words will crack and break.

I want to grab on to those words
and hold them tight. But I can't.
The guilt and worry and sadness
I feel about everything
that's happened won't let me.

"Stay and let us help you. Let us be your family.
Don't you see, Lauren? We love you."

"But, you don't trust me," I say.

"Maybe at first, we didn't," Josh says.
"Because of things your mom said.
But we do now. Let us prove it to you.
Stay and let us show you."

"Don't feel sorry for me," I say,
tears pooling in my eyes.
"I don't want your pity."

"No," Josh says. "This is not pity.
This is so much more. Just ask the kids,
who are downstairs,
wishing and hoping you
don't get on that plane."

I think of the three of them, huddled
together, wanting a happy ending,
like one of their storybooks.

"But . . . my mom. And my brother."

Erica takes my hand. Holds it.
"Your mom will be okay.
We'll make her understand.
And we can visit your brother
as much as you want."

It's like a whirlwind of thoughts
in my brain and I'm in the middle,
trying not to get swept
away in the wrong direction.

"I really want to go to college."

"Of course you do," Josh says. "And you should."

"I'll get you lots of books to read.
About applications and financial aid."

I smile through the tears.
"It's not too late? To apply?"

"Not at all," he says. "And we'll help you."

"I know it probably sounds weird,
but I think I want to study birds.
Like, I'm fascinated by them, and maybe
I can't make a living doing that,
but I'd like to find out. To learn more."

"Going to college is a great way
to explore your interests," Josh says.

"Did you know we have a pair of mourning doves
nesting in the bushes in our backyard?" Erica asks.

"It's almost winter," I say. "Do they stay here?"

"Yes," she says. "They don't migrate."
They stay here. Right here.

"Please, Lauren," Josh says.
"Stay with us."

Maybe I had it all wrong.
Maybe I'm a mourning dove.

Maybe I am
supposed
to stay.

114 : Colby

I KEEP hearing the words I said to Lauren.

What you want matters most of all.

How can I be such a hypocrite? Telling her that, and yet not believing it for myself?

Lauren doesn't have to go, and yet she is, because she thinks that's what she's supposed to do.

I'm so angry, I can hardly see straight as I drive.

I can't make Lauren do the right thing. I can't make her stay. But I can do the right thing for myself. It's so obvious now, what I'm supposed to believe in when this game tonight is over.

I'm supposed to believe in *myself.*

That's why Coach put that ahead of the team and the season. When everything else is over and done with, I still have myself. I still have to believe in me. And believe that what I want for my life matters.

I call my dad and put it on speaker.

"Colby! Good, I'm so glad you called before you left. I know you must be nervous, but it's going to be —"

"Dad," I interrupt him. "Listen. I'm calling to tell you something. I know you're not going to like it, but I need to get this off my chest. This will be my last game. After tonight, it's over. I'm done."

"What do you mean you're done?"

"I mean, I'm done with football. I don't want to play next year. I want to go to Whitman College in Washington, and I want to study civil engineering. I've read up on Whitman, Dad, and it's a good school. Not too far from home, either."

"Son, look, let's not talk about this now. Your emotions are running high because of this game, and that's understandable. It's okay. Relax. Don't worry about college right now. We have a lot of time to decide."

"No, Dad. I've decided. Me. Because it's my decision. Please, you have to understand, I don't want to play anymore. I love my team, and yeah, I love what I've learned being a part of that team. But I'm ready to move on. And I need you to be okay with that. Please? Please, tell me you're okay with that. Because I can't stand the thought of disappointing you." Tears stream down my face. "Please, Dad."

"How are you going to pay for it if you don't have a football scholarship?"

"I don't know right this minute, but I know people do it all the time. I'll figure it out."

"You make it sound so easy, Colby. Private colleges are expensive. And besides all of that, you have talent, son. Real talent. Do you know how many kids would kill to have what you have? I'm just not sure you're thinking clearly on this."

I pull into the school parking lot and park my truck. Players are streaming out of the school, ready to go have the time of their lives. And then there's the line of cheerleaders, Meghan and all the rest, standing by the bus. I'm sure they've planned some kind of send-off that we'll never forget. We're stars after all.

But I'm so tired of being a star in a jersey.

I just want to be me.

"Colby? You still there? Look, let's talk about this tomorrow, okay? You have a game to play. Concentrate on that."

I've probably done all I can do for now. I realize this isn't a fight that I can win with just one phone call.

"Yeah. You're right. We'll talk tomorrow. But I need you to know, I've thought about it a long time. I just . . . I didn't want to disappoint you, that's why it's been so hard for me to tell you until now."

He doesn't say anything for a moment. I'm about to say good-bye, when he says, "So what's the deal with the civil engineering? You hoping to design bridges or something?"

"Yeah. That's exactly what I want to do."

"You know, your gram loves bridges."

"I know she does."

"She's so proud of you," he says. "She told me just last night how proud she is of the man you've become."

"I'm glad you guys will all be there tonight."

He pauses again, like he's trying to find the right words. "And look, I want you to know, I'm proud of you too. Whatever happens, that will never change."

I exhale as I lean down and rest my forehead on the steering wheel.

"Thanks," I tell him.

"Have fun tonight," he says. "Take it all in. It's a night you'll never forget."

I think of what's just happened with Lauren. I think about seeing Benny. And most of all, about being on that field one last time with my friends, my teammates.

And I know, for once, my dad is exactly right.

115 | Lauren

BIG BLUE sky.
Wide open road.
Cars heading out of town.

I understand now.

It's more than a game.
It's about being a part of something.

It feels good to be a part of something.

There is nowhere else I want to be
than in this car, going to this game.

I don't care that much about football.

I never have.
Still, I care about being a part of this night.

A part of something outside myself.

Creek parties.
Bake sales.
Aimless driving in the country.

I understand now.

Small-town life is
loving the wide roads one day
and wanting to leave and never
look back the next.

But you accept that's how it is,
because you're a part of something.

And because . . . it's home.

116 : Colby

BEFORE THE game, Coach gathers us in the locker room. If he's nervous, he doesn't show it. His voice is calm. Reassuring. I suddenly realize how much I'm going to miss that voice. His talks. The incredible leadership he's provided.

I sure am going to miss him.

"Tonight is your night, gentlemen," Coach says.

"You have worked hard to be here.

"You have endured physical and emotional pain, beyond any you could have imagined, and proved you are the best of the best.

"You've made it. You're here. And I know you're going to go out there and play harder than you've ever played before. So all I want to say right now, to each and every one of you, is enjoy it. Look up at those people, cheering for you, and take it in. Feel their love for you and this team and our small town, and play with full, proud, happy hearts.

"I believe in you.

"They believe in you.

"But what got you here is the belief in yourself. You never gave up. And that right there is the true sign of a winner, regardless of what happens out there tonight."

He smiles and turns around. Waves at someone. And from the door that leads outside to the field, in walks Benny.

As soon as we see him, we yell like the place is on fire. He's got a helmet on his head. Not a football helmet, but a special protective helmet. He comes in slowly, all by himself, a grin as wide as the Willamette River on his face.

Soon, we're yelling his name. "Benny, Benny, Benny."

Coach lets it go on for a minute, then motions with his hands for us to quiet down, so we do. And then he turns to Benny and says, "You have something to say to us, don't you, Lewis?"

He looks at us, holds his fists up in the air, and yells, "I believe!"

It is loud and strong and true.

"I believe!" we yell back.

And in that moment, through all the mixed emotions I have about everything that's happened in the past twenty-four hours, I *do* believe.

117 Lauren

TEARS WELL up
when the blue-and-gold
Eagles fly onto the field
and through the big
paper banner.

The crowd explodes
as all the players turn
and look at their fans
in the stands.

I jump up and down,
waving, but I know
the chance of Colby seeing
me is nearly zero.
He's too far away,
and there are just
too many of us here tonight.

First quarter,
everyone's a bundle
of nerves. A couple of big

mistakes put us
down by seven.

Second quarter,
Colby catches two
impressive passes,
one of them getting us
close to the end zone.

When we score
on the next play,
it's a hug-fest
with me and the little ones.

Tied at halftime.

118 : Colby

IN THE locker room, Coach comes down hard on us for the stupid mistakes we made in the first half.

"Too many lost opportunities!" he says. "And if you don't find your focus and play the way I know you can play, this entire game will be a lost opportunity."

He talks about courage and teamwork. About dedication and drive. About putting it all on the line right now, because this is it. This is all we've got.

"This is the end of the story," he tells us. "Right here. It's up to you how you want to write it. How you want to be remembered. But even more importantly, how you want to remember this night for the rest of your lives."

He finishes up, and we take a minute for ourselves before we break and hit the field.

I'm trying to focus on what I need to do when we go out there again, but I can't stop thinking about the surprise I got a little while ago. As we were running into the locker room at the half, I looked up at the crowd, trying to spot my dad sitting with Gram and Grandpa.

I couldn't find them.

But I saw four blue-and-gold hats, all in a row. I'd know those awesome hats anywhere.

My heart feels like a balloon about to pop, because she's here. Whether she's going to the airport afterward, who knows, but she's here now. She couldn't stay away.

This must have been how Superman felt when he found out Lois Lane had feelings for him.

I bet Superman would have been a helluva football player.

119 Lauren

COLBY IS the star
of the second half.

It's like he's been
gifted with superpowers.

He catches
pass
after pass
after pass.

We are
on our feet
the entire
time because
the air is full
of excitement
and hope.

Just like
Colby said.

It feels good
to believe and hope.

As the clock
counts down
the final seconds,
we count with it.

Ten

    I will

Nine

    never forget

Eight

    this

Seven

    night

Six

    and how

Five

    good

Four

    it felt

Three

    to

Two

    belong

One

It feels
so good to win.

I look at
my aunt and uncle,
arms high,
cheering loud,
and my little cousins
dancing around.

All I can think is,
what a team.

What a *great* team
I'm on.

120 Colby

WE DID it. We took state.

There is running, yelling, and group hugging, and then, when I get a chance, I stand there for a moment and take it all in.

The cheering blue-and-gold crowd.

The final score in bright lights.

The feeling that anything truly is possible, with the right people by your side.

I don't know what tomorrow will bring. All I know is right now, despite everything that's happened this season, we did what we set out to do.

It's amazing to know I was a part of something the town will talk about forever. And it's something *good*.

Finally. Something good.

If someone in the stands needed some hope that things will be all right, they got a good, healthy dose of it tonight.

All of us did.

121 Lauren

THE EAGLES soar.

It's the end
of the game.

The end of
the season.

The end of
awe-inspiring dedication.

And yet,
in so many ways,
it's only the beginning.

They worked so hard
to get here, which makes it
all the sweeter.

I did too.

The journey had
its ups and downs,

but here we are,
looking out at the horizon,
dreaming about what
comes next.

The Eagles soar,
and the town soars with them.

I get it now.

It's not just a game.
It's life, played out on the field.

And whether you win or lose,
the important thing is
who you are when it's over.

122 : Colby

AFTER THE celebratory Gatorade is poured all over Coach and we've told every one of our opponents "Good game" as nice sportsmen do, we scatter to find our families, who stream onto the field.

Before I look for mine, though, I make my way to Benny and give him a big hug. We don't say a word. We don't need to. It's a night to be happy, but there is a hint of sadness here too. Benny should have been out there with us, and we both feel that loss. I'm guessing we probably always will.

"It's so good to see you," I tell him. "Man, I've missed you."

"No mushy stuff, Pynes."

"See you tomorrow?"

He smiles. And sounding just like my old pal Benny, he says, "You can count on that."

My dad and grandparents find me, going on and on about how well I played and what a fantastic game it was. I give them each a quick hug and tell them there's something I have to do before it gets too late.

"I understand," Dad says. "This is your night. Go revel in it."

I don't know what he's thinking I'm going to do, but whatever it is, he's way off.

I scan the bleachers for her, hoping they didn't jet off yet. I look and look, but I don't see them.

"Crap," I whisper under my breath.

"Pynes?" Temple says. "You okay? Come on, man, it's just about trophy time."

"Yeah, all right," I say. "Be there in a minute."

I scan one more time for the blue-and-gold hats, but they're gone.

She's gone. I've missed her.

I turn back around, toward the center of the field, my chest aching like I took a hit there. But of course, that's not why it hurts.

And then I hear "Colby!" from far away.

I look left and right, but I don't see her. Where is she?

"Behind you," she calls out.

I turn around and there she is, on the field, walking toward me.

I start running to her, and as soon as I do, she's running too.

When we meet, I throw my helmet on the ground, pick her up, and lift her high. She laughs and laughs. As I lower her down, I stop when we're eye level and hold her there. Then I kiss her like I've wanted to kiss her since the first day we met.

With everything I have. With everything I am.

There is no question about this girl. I am all in, one hundred percent.

She tastes salty, like popcorn. Or Bugles.

And suddenly, I'm laughing, remembering how we met and how far we've come.

"What?" she asks, smiling. "What is it?"

"I'm just so glad you're here," I whisper as her feet touch the ground.

"It's a two-for-one, you know."

I give her a funny look. "What is?"

"My being here."

"How so?"

"Well, I came to watch you play *and* I came to tell you I'm not leaving. My aunt and uncle asked me to stay and so, I am. They're going to help me get into college and everything."

My jaw drops to the turf, and then I'm picking her up again and spinning her around and around, until I finally stop, both of us dizzy.

I kiss her one more time.

"Come on," I say. "There's someone I want you to meet. I was thinking maybe the three of us could go out tomorrow night, to Angie's Restaurant. That way I can spend time with both of you."

She smiles. "You are the king of two-for-ones, aren't you?"

I laugh. "I probably am. You okay with that?"

She squeezes my hand. "Totally okay." She stops walking, and points across the field. "Wait, Colby, the trophy. Shouldn't you be over there?"

I shake my head. Benny's just up ahead. I walk faster.

I don't need a trophy to tell me I've won.